A Trip
to Salt Lake

For our mother and Stanley (Lloyd).

...IF THERE IS NO ONE
YOU WOULD GIVE YOUR LIFE FOR
YOU DON'T QUITE KNOW LIFE
AND
YOU WON'T QUITE KNOW LOVE.

GIANMARCO--SACRIFICE

1.

FROM SAN FRANCISCO AIRPORT—BY GREYHOUND—IT IS TWO hours to Santa Cruz. Enroute eucalyptus trees, two bus stops, then flat land—artichoke land, with trailer homes and parked motorcycles. The road climbs, pines rise, their shadows click the sun on and off through bus windows to glimpses of the ocean, gulls circling; from the highway small houses, a green cement building marked *Palm Reader*, a stark-white Unitarian church with a spacious parking lot, a store offering surfboards, another bicycles. Many cats lounging, for they are fed and happy. Last a handsome, well-kept bridge that leads to town.

I was on my way to visit Lloyd, my step-father, now widowed, my mother had passed away three years ago. Lloyd now eighty-three.

The Greyhound rounded a corner, then slipped in front of the peach-colored Santa Cruz depot. It pulled to a stop at the passenger entrance. The bus was full. We were a mixed bag that lined the aisle, a human mixture of Santa Cruz: parents, kids themselves, with sleeping toddlers in their arms, passive-looking Mexicans, senior citizens, and a few people spaced out on drugs. Completing the line were older women—and myself, early-thirties. In front of me were two bearded young men with ID bracelets—Vietnam vets—eyes that have seen it all, eyes that don't forget, eyes that we have viewed time and again in newspaper photos, therefore we, who have not been there, are not allowed to forget. They can be recognized, thus reminders, on a Greyhound bus. All a quiet group, no one in a hurry to get off. As for me, I had conflicting feelings about my trips to Santa Cruz, a place I had always been attached to having vacationed here as a child now sobered without my mother's presence. Her death had not changed our visiting habits. Nina, my sister and I still came twice a year to see Lloyd, he dividing his time to stay with each of us over the Christmas holidays.

I stood in the aisle waiting my turn, still wondering about the words I had yet to find that would convince him it was time to move—my mission this visit. For one he often complained about climbing the stairs to his condo front door. Outside stairs that led up to the second floor. He was not the type to acknowledge weaknesses—a long bachelorhood had taught him how to deal privately with emotions. And he was stubborn, with an old Chicago toughness, feelings expressed through action rather than words. Each year Nina and I mentioned his moving near Nina or near me. Each time he became impatient with us.

"I'm fine in our house," he still referred to his home as *ours*: *our* bedroom, *our* kitchen, *we keep the flour here, Margo*; when on visits, he reminds me of the location of ingredients.

Breaking with the past? In Lloyd's case, leaving his apartment and memories without our mother? It would be hard. Nina and I had discussed this many times. We had talked about roots, the elderly, and should they move (Lloyd and our mother had been living in Santa Cruz over twenty years) and did years in one place tip the scale over practical reasons for leaving?

The driver waited next to the bus and told each one of us to watch our step. His was a cheerful, vigorous voice, hopeful, as if it were his duty to inject life into the odd mixture of travelers, none of us holding the future of the world in our hands. When our mother was alive, she and Lloyd would wait for me inside the depot, right next to the entrance so I would see them when the bus emptied. Now, when I arrived, Lloyd, ever practical, waited in the parking lot across from the entrance. This I sometimes forgot finding the depot empty. Was he ill, I worried upon not finding him. The scene would invariably play out: my alarm because he was not in the depot, then remembering that I'd find him, keys dangling from his hand, standing by the car in the parking lot.

All the suitcases were grouped inside the depot. I picked out mine and headed through the automatic doors to outside. I looked up. He was standing by the car in the parking lot, a small man, car keys dangling from his hand, sunlight reflecting from his glasses, a light breeze feathering his white hair. We both smiled at each other. He was dressed for the occasion, dapper in light blue and beige plaid slacks and a beige sports jacket, a blue triangle of a handkerchief poking up smartly from the jacket pocket. It was almost dusk and cool, but for Lloyd, a light jacket was sufficient. He rarely got cold.

"You should wear a coat, Lloyd," I would say when we went out in foggy weather, he as usual in a sports jacket, at the most a light raincoat. And though he always claimed he was fine as he was, I never learned to stop nagging him. We embraced, and he asked me if I had a good trip. I worried he sometimes considered my coming a duty, a sacrifice, and he didn't want to put me out. I would have liked to say life was about caring—speaking for Nina and myself. What's more I looked forward to coming. But I wouldn't say it. He would prefer not to delve into any kind of sentimental reasoning. We kept our conversations on another level, anything less profound might be exchanging stories about the past—Salt Lake memories, important to us. He had shed many tears at our mother's funeral, but outwardly it was over. Sorrowing after her death remained private.

Lloyd opened the trunk of the car, the next step to insist on lifting my suitcase himself and setting it inside, always prompting a little discussion about who would do it. A point of pride? Not only for gallantry was second nature to him: he opened doors for women—most of the time I thoughtlessly burst from the car, catching him mid-way in circling around to open it for me—and he always walked on the curb-side of the street. I picked up the suitcase and swiftly put it in the trunk. To have the last say, he reached in and straightened it. I saw there were two boxes of Presto Logs settled in back with a case of Cokes and wondered how long they had been there. I imagined he had put that duty off since there were those stairs.

The ride was short. With the still new without our mother relationship. It was rarely that way when Nina and I were young for they both seemed to occupy space together. I had never looked at him singularly as a person. Result, protectiveness on my part, he now a widower. But a Chicagoan. A member of those who lived in the shadow of the Al Capone time and who survived and thrived on realism: what couldn't be changed *there* were other directions.

My thoughts that took place on a two-hour bus trip to Santa Cruz. That Lloyd has never changed. That what one sees has always been: he, owner of a past of independence, one who has always been fine with it. Yet there are others, namely Nina and myself, with our feelings to convince him to change his life—better for him—or us? Age, as a convincer, is the unspoken word. A reminder to be left out. Its persistence, its duty to perform, is not a qualification for vocalizing.

Our mother was forty-four when she married Lloyd. She, Nina and I had been living in Salt Lake for two years. Salt Lake was our mother's hometown, and we had moved there from California soon after our father had died. Lloyd was eight years older than our mother. Before their marriage, he had been living downtown at the Hotel Utah for fifteen years. He worked as a film distributor for Metro Goldwyn Mayer. They met at a party, the story goes, fell in love while dancing their first dance together to the song "Some Enchanted Evening." They had been a couple well-matched. Even physically, both small people, both with clear blue eyes, and I never heard a cross word between them and I never heard him call her by name. It was always "Honey."

For her he was always Lloyd. As it was for Nina and myself. I wondered if he ever had a nickname. I could never imagine the name "Lloyd" attached to a child. This, Nina and I would laugh about. But if we laughed, it was only when we first met him, when we were a well-knit family of three and a male friend of our mother's was an intruder, a threat. Selfish at that age with no thoughts to their happiness.

We crossed the bridge over the San Lorenzo River. The river was high, the color of wet wood, and there were large tree branches in it hardly blending. I knew the cause of its state had been a rainstorm a month ago that had lasted for three days. We talked on the phone often, and Lloyd later told me about the storm—after the phones were working once more. He told me how the telephone poles had been blown down in Watsonville, a town close by, how some houses farther north had slipped down hills with mud slides and how lucky he had been to be sitting peacefully at home in front of the fire with a store just across the street that delivered groceries. No way would he have ventured out, he said. Listening to him on the phone, I pictured him alone, cut off from the world due to the storm and wondered if he felt lonely, if in the long run as a Chicagoan, the bachelor years at the Hotel Utah were indeed enough to sustain him.

Those thoughts provided some weight to a question in urging him to leave his home of twenty years.

He said that the river had been much higher than it was now due to the storm, in some parts it had even run over.

"At least it kept the hippies from sleeping under the bridge," he said, not joking. He never joked about hippies in Santa Cruz. He disliked them with a passion.

"But perhaps there's less of a problem compared to what it used to be?" I suggested, trying to sound positive, though knew it to be true. "It seemed to me that on my last visit there weren't as many hippies as in the past years. For sure I saw less children on the streets." Silently remembering one period where you couldn't tell who the kids belonged to. They mingled in the adult world belonging to everybody.

"Oh, hell, Margo,"one of his favorite swear-words, that particular one firmly rooted from his film days, "the kids probably grew up. The hippies are still here. None of us ever go to town anymore." *Us* were the Santa Cruzers, who considered themselves apart from the *others*—interlopers-strangers. "We all go to San Francisco or San Jose." Amused I wondered about the word *we* since I knew he only went to those two places to depart from the airport to visit Nina and myself. Lloyd had always been perfectly happy in his home, and I would say much of it was due to his traveling when he worked in Salt Lake for Metro Goldwyn Mayer.

"They're a bunch of No-Gooders, that's what they are. Hanging around in the streets, a lot of then so drugged, they can't walk straight. They haven't done a lick of work in their lives."

He told me again the story of when, before the Santa Cruz take-over, the hippies used to fill the streets of Carmel until the local people banded together and forced them out, one method being water, fire hoses from the fire department. He had many stories. Now with age, he reached back, memories strong. Ever the practical man, he was not one to exaggerate, proof was the stories never changed. He repeated what he heard or what had happened just as he knew it. Of course I knew the Carmel hippy story very well, as his Chicago ones, but I never tired of them.

Lloyd, born in Chicago, lived there during the twenties, a period of glamour and excitement that–through his descriptions—always held a fascination for me. He told me how he used to wear spats and carry a cane—everyone had canes then, he had five or six of them, all very fancy. He had one story where he shook Al Capone's hand. They were both in the same restaurant. Lloyd went up to him and put out his hand.

"Hello, Mr. Capone, my name is Lloyd Edwards." Al Capone shook his hand and said he was glad to meet him. Not shy about some things, Lloyd has never been reluctant to approach a famous person and shake the hand. He shook Ernest Hemingway's hand on the porch of a lodge in Sun Valley and President Truman's hand in the foyer of the Hotel Utah. There were secret service agents all over—so goes the President Truman story—and Lloyd went up to one and asked if he could shake the president's hand. He was told he could, but only if the president came his way. He waited with the others. Soon the president and his daughter appeared. They were walking in his direction. When the President was close enough, Lloyd stepped forward and asked him if he could shake his hand.

"You sure can," said the President. Lloyd shook his hand and then his daughter's.

To my question on shaking hands, I asked him why Capone's? The big boss of crime in your city? To shake HIS hand?

"You can tell a person by a handshake," he said. "What the person wants, who the person is right then. I'm always curious."

"And Capone?"

"His hand was like ice. I'll always remember it. Like the temperature of a cold gun. Right then that thought came to me—a cold gun. Then I never thought about it again. Not worth it."

"I've had a good life, Margo," he once told me. "I loved Chicago—those were the good old days. As long as you kept on the right side of the tracks. Capone and his gang hung around another part of the city. Banks and so on. They didn't affect us. Ballroom dancing was the big thing then. Dinner and dancing. I loved staying at The Hotel Utah all those years. But the best part of all of it was your mother."

I was twelve when Lloyd formally entered our family. Nina was ten. It was a family wedding. The four of us rode the train to Reno, Nina and I standing behind them in a room of the courthouse while they were married by a Justice of the Peace. After that we all went to San Francisco and stayed at the Sir Francis Drake Hotel. I don't believe I ever once resented him after their marriage. At that age, I did not think about it while at that age one could. It was life, although not a philosophical thought of mine at the time. For one thing, as far as I was concerned, it was a relief. I had taken on the household chores—our mother worked—and did not care if I ever laid eyes on our worn metal carpet sweeper again, whose tired mechanical movements to this day echo in my ears. And he never interfered with the raising of us. A wise choice for he knew better than to intrude in the task of raising two girls, one on the brink of adolescence. Not the same as ballroom dancing in Chicago, nor the life of independence at the Hotel Utah. Never married. Suddenly sharing.

Because Lloyd was eight years older than our mother, it seemed the natural course that he would be the first to go. Another reason was his addiction to Coca-Cola. Though he smoked, it was the Coke habit that carried ominous implications—cartons of empty bottles rattling in the car to return for full ones, as permanent a fixture as the car upholstery. Nature does not tolerate predictions of life expectancies, and so it was our mother who left this world first. She died in her sleep, in the arms of Lloyd who was sleeping beside her.

We were silent as we turned into his street, then the wide circular driveway. Bordering the circular driveway were three two-level condo buildings, and Lloyd lived in one of the middle buildings on the second level. Thus the stairs to climb.

"Wait here a minute, Lloyd, in front, and I'll unload."

He stayed in the car without protest. Last year I had to argue with him, and he won because he wanted to park and take the suitcase out himself. Roll it over to the stairs. I brought it up myself. This time I also sneaked out the Presto Logs. Figured he already had a few Cokes in the fridge. He pulled away and eased the car into his space inside the car port. I was waiting for him at his front door as he slowly climbed the steps.

"Oh, for Pete's sake, you also brought up the logs?"

I watched him fit the key into the door, then he swung the door open and stood aside to let me pass.

My mother's presence or her absence greeted me as usual. It was swift and clean and powerful. It held me at the door, kept me in place for a few seconds. Seeing familiar things and not our mother in the middle of them had not ceased to startle me. I could still not quite get used to it. I suspect that Lloyd never quite could either, or at least sensed my feelings, for he would have an immediate comment, a buffer, to avoid an awkwardness.

"Well, you know where to go. Yell if you need anything."

He headed for the kitchen. On the first night of my visit, he always fixed the meal: steak, baked potatoes, and frozen peas, a bottle of wine. For dessert there would be ice cream. After dinner he did the dishes. Even when I cooked. It was the only exercise he got, he said. Without mentioning the stairs. The rest of the cleaning was left up to two women who came every three weeks. For one hour. I once tried to convince him to have them stay longer; what could be done in an hour?

"Two in the house? An hour's just fine." Case closed. For I knew better than to pursue certain subjects.

I unpacked my suitcase in the guestroom. It was a pleasant room with lots of light from a skylight and a window that looked out on the balcony; the beige shag carpet added an air of coziness to it. The bedspread had become faded from the skylight, and I thought I should change it but knew I wouldn't. Lloyd didn't care, Nina and I being the only persons who spent time in the room, except the two ladies who cleaned it.

I picked up the framed photograph that sat on the dresser and looked at it as I always did when I arrived in the room. It was a picture of me in Grand Canyon, in my uniform, standing in front of one of the cabins I cleaned. Lloyd had found the summer job for me through his many contacts. The one of Nina, in shorts, standing next to our cream-colored Packard replaced my photo upon her visits. Our mother's doing. The way of welcoming us. Lloyd continued it.

I positioned the photo back in its place and wandered into the living room, opened the sliding glass doors, and stepped out onto the wide balcony. The view was Santa Cruz, the hills surrounding it that now, at dusk, had become a chain of rounded shadows. A light breeze brought with it the heady perfume of eucalyptus and honeysuckle. I watched the lights of Santa Cruz flicker on until they became a solid carpet of yellow up to the hills. On the crest of one was the old white church that against the darkening sky seemed suspended.

Nina and I each had done research for a retirement home, she in Boston, myself, close to mine in the suburbs of Washington D.C. I brought the information with me. The buildings were similar in the sense the Boston one a yellow brick, in my area a soft red brick. Nina's had many trees in front, and mine, flowers and a wide green lawn. There were floor plans similar to where Lloyd now lived. In the modern kitchen, he could cook or eat in the dining room of the complex. Living in either Washington or Boston, he would be able to visit Nina or myself when he chose; we would visit him. It was not called a *retirement home* but Community Place.

"It's an apartment, Lloyd, an independent apartment. It's called Community Place because that's what it is, a community. There's a beautiful dining room, in case you decide you don't want to fix your own meals, and a well-stocked library where a few times a week are lectures and bridge games"— Lloyd, an excellent bridge player. This I would say to him. I wondered now if I should leave the pamphlets I brought with me on a table to rest casually. I laughed at myself over the idea. It reminded me of my mother's *casual* way of teaching me the facts of life: little magazines I would find set on the edge of tables. Little magazines that remained untouched. I discounted the idea.

I shut my eyes and took a deep breath of the Santa Cruz air. I was lucky to be able to come in the spring due to my work as a school teacher and vacation. I loved teaching, my students on the brink of adolescence, minds young and open. This time I was able to add more vacation to my trip, lucky enough to find a substitute. Time needed to talk to Lloyd about moving. Nina, being a nurse, came in autumn when she could find a substitute in the hospital where she worked.

I thought of the two Vietnam vets on the bus today, which brought me back to Devon. The man and marriage I left two years ago, Dev and I meeting for the first time at a reception for those who were to depart for Vietnam.

Tall, blond Devon with gentle brown eyes that looked at me with deep honesty. We were married when he returned. A happy marriage, during the period without children, but we had planned on their coming.

The reason I left Dev had its origin in a bar. We had been to the movies that evening. After the movies, we stopped at a bar for a beer, and it was there that Dev ran into one of his war buddies. His name was Gary. If it hadn't been that fateful meeting with Gary, I would still be married to Devon. I will always remember what Gary looked like, the meeting that changed my life. Well, also that of Dev's.

Neither one of them could believe their good luck at coming upon each other. They ordered another round of beer, and the two men got to talking about their experiences. They had both flown helicopters during the war and sometimes had gone out in the same one. They had many stories, some amusing, others close calls, "and a miracle we are sitting here," said Gary. Dev had never talked about the war, therefore what I was hearing was the first time.

As much as I had tried, I could never remember if it was Devon or Gary who launched into the description of the time they were flying the helicopter and shot all the people below. Dev said he thought there must have been about twenty or twenty-five, though Gary thought it was less. I asked them if they, Dev and Gary, were scared, as I imagined the people below were pointing guns, maybe even shooting at their helicopter. Out of fear for him, I grabbed his hand.

"Hell no," said Dev. "They were just ordinary people. They didn't have guns *then*, but they sure were going to get them."

"But why would you shoot them if they were unarmed and you were in a helicopter and could get away?"

"Just to make sure they'd never get those guns. Kids like those can be pretty manipulative."

I had not understood. "I had assumed the people were all soldiers," I said. Out of uniform, because he said *ordinary* people, but still I envisioned all soldiers. In any case, an enemy. But kids?

"Listen, every one of those people, even if not in uniform, was still considered a soldier. An *enemy* let's say."

Of course I knew I had misunderstood, but I just asked anyway, and what did he mean by kids?

"A lot of them were kids, that's all."

"You mean you shot them?"

"Yeah, you bet we shot them."

"How old were they?"

" I dunno. Ten, maybe twelve."

"How could you? Children!" I slipped my hands from his, now foreign to me.

"Come on, Margo. They were *kids*, not children."

"What's the difference?" I asked angrily.

"So have it your way. *Children*. It doesn't change anything. These are kids who grow up fast. Killers. They may have looked innocent, but we couldn't take a chance. If we didn't get them, they would have gotten us some other time. Maybe I was saving my own life right then." He leaned over and kissed me. "Then we would have never known each other, did you ever think of that?"

"What were they doing when you killed them?"

He and Gary exchanged blank looks.

"What were they doing, Dev?" his friend asked. "You were the one who spotted them down the road."

"You mean you were ABOVE them when you found they were a threat, but in reality, they were down the road?"

"Jesus, Margo," and he ran his hand through his blond hair. "Let's change the subject. Why are you so interested in something in the past?"

"All I remember," said Gary, "is when we pointed our guns at them, they began to run. And looking back at us scared."

"Well, they should have been," said Dev.

I rocked my beer glass back and forth and watched the foam roll like a small wave. I took a drink. It was unpleasantly warm.

"Did you feel bad after you did it? Guilty, I mean?" Looking for some last saving grace in the heart of my husband.

Both of them were quiet.

Dev then said, "We're talking about the war, Margo. You can't go around feeling guilty about everyone you kill. Anyway, when you think about it, a bullet put through a person from a distance, well, it's like you're not the one who did it. It's the damn bullet, not you. Very impersonal. You haven't touched the person. It's not the same as going up and putting a knife through the person. Not me, I could never do that. A bullet? You do it and leave. All over in seconds. You see people fall around you, but it's just so distant. Guns? They do all the work for you. And let me add this, in some countries, kids marry at twelve."

"In my country, *our* country, twelve is still children and they do not marry."

I stared at Dev, my husband with the gentle brown eyes, honest eyes, and there was an awkward silence. I had become a thorn. If I had gone home, they would have taken up talking where they had left off before the subject of the shooting incident. As it was, the two exchanged addresses and said goodbye to each other.

That was the beginning. Or the beginning toward a change in my marriage. If only later on Dev could have shown a small sign of guilt. Something over what he had done. But the guilt nurtured was mine. Maybe someone else, someone with higher morals, a better person than myself, would have easily lost her love for the person who committed such a dastardly deed. I did not admire myself. I wondered about my own principles.

But eventually those principles tipped the scale.

One day, while preparing dinner, I saw Dev out on the front lawn playing touch football with a group of neighborhood children. They had stopped, and he was explaining something to them. They were all standing around him, and he was holding the football high in the air above them. They were listening to him intently, their hero. Yet it was reciprocal. He wasn't playing the hero, I could see he sincerely liked the kids. He put down the ball and tousled the hair of one of them; the boy looked at Devon, eyes full of trust. The trust of one who did not know mortal enemies the way kids, unarmed kids, looked. The whole scene made me sick. I imagined Dev in a helicopter above the children—not white children, for I had come to believe it was race with him—they looking up innocently, he then gunning them down. I could picture them running hysterically, blood flowing. A deep hatred for what he had done, for what he was showing now, his unabashed caring for them, the hypocrisy so profound that I had to go lie down. I knew then I did not want him as a father for my children.

Later, without another word, I packed my things and left. I did not return.

For a time, Dev was heartbroken and couldn't understand any of it. Not even the long letter I had written explaining how I could not live with a man who had done what he had done and still not feel guilt. With time he became resigned—I did not love him enough; I did not care that he very possibly was saving his own life by shooting the kids. He deserved a stronger love.

A year later, he married.

My mother's death allowed her to avoid the pain of our divorce. Lloyd was very sorry because he liked Devon. Later he told me I had done the right thing and I did what I had to do, and he respected me for it.

"Life can turn on a dime," he told me, "and let me add, with only a finger on the wheel. So be it." Vintage Lloyd.

Lloyd was pulling the cork from the bottle of wine as I came later into the kitchen.

"I bought white wine. Is white alright?"

"Sure," I said. He rarely drank, and if he did, it was a martini before dinner. I appreciated his buying it for me, he knew I liked it with meals. I saw it was Pinot Grigio.

"That's my favorite. Pinot Grigio is a very good, dry wine."

"Oh, I didn't know. Is it?"

As he was not much of a drinker, he knew little about wine. There were times when I was not so lucky in his choices.

"How do you want your steak?"

He was peering into the oven, poking the steaks under the grill.

"Well done."

"Then go sit down and pour yourself some wine," he commanded.

He set the wine in a silver wine holder on the dinner table, patties of butter, perfect squares, formed a neat circle on a plate. The wire butter cutter was purchased after Mother died, the only thing in his life Lloyd had ever bought on his own for their house. It was the way they used to serve butter at the Hotel Utah he reminded me, when on my last visit and I saw it for the first time. To this day, I will never know how he came upon it and if he had gone with great purpose to a kitchen store to search one out. I did not ask.

I sipped the wine, remembering those meals at the hotel, the bottles of wine under tables because it was Mormon owned and one had to bring one's own liquor—what's more keep it out of sight. After they were married, we spent many nights eating there while our kitchen was being enlarged: hot turkey sandwiches, Nina's favorite, steaks, spinach in separate bowls that I always pushed aside because they were watery. And always the patties of butter that made an even circle on the plate. Yes, now on the dinner table in Santa Cruz they looked familiar.

Fog had rolled in during the night. It had wrapped the city in its soft, gray blanket, so I could barely make out the houses below us. Knowing I liked the beach, Lloyd forecasted it would burn off, though I said it didn't matter. I'd go to town. For now we went grocery shopping, our usual routine when I arrived. To do this, Lloyd took the automobile and we drove to the store across the street. He never did like to walk. I continued to be alarmed that at eighty-three he now drove at all, mostly my questioning the wisdom of it. I felt I should say something, maybe suggest he sell the car, use taxis and delivery services, then we'd drive off and I would see his reflexes were as good as mine. Nina and I agreed he owed this to those years on the road when he worked for Metro Goldwyn Mayer. This meant going around Utah and Nevada—his territory—in his cream-colored Packard sedan—a make he still claims was better than any car—talking to the owners of movie theaters. Bingham, St. George, Spanish Fork, Ogden, they all had meaning to me, the places he traveled, then came home and talked about them. Spanish Fork held the nicest movie house compared to all the others in Utah, and he didn't have to tell us— it already known by the locals that St. George had an institution for the mentally ill, along with the town having large houses for those in the Mormon Church who had more than one wife. We learned the names of the theater owners, who belonged to each town, the movies that played well, and also where he ran into such-and-such crony our mother knew on his trip; the restaurants that served the best food, and how in Spanish Fork there were plans to build a new movie house to fit the new jumbo screens.

During the next few days, the fog lifted only in late afternoon. Lloyd and I spent time on errands in the car: the post office, the bank, the store with barrels of dried fruit, well-known for their succulence in California. On my own later, I strolled into Santa Cruz, visited the bookstores and a favorite that sold Deco objects. They were crammed everywhere: appliances—that one could literally toss out the window and they would remain intact, chunky Royal typewriters, that one had to work up to over forty words a minute to be hired as a secretary, wood table-radios, a presence in a room decades ago.

But Lloyd was right about the hippie scene and that it had not changed. There were still many, although the *hippie* had been replaced by the word *drug addict* and who looked as if his/her days were numbered. In contrast, as if bent on ignoring the problem, the town was clean and pretty, lined with trees, boutiques and cafes, two large department stores, and on a corner was a museum regarding the history of Santa Cruz.

The sharp morning light of April cut through the skylight and woke me, an announcement of no fog. I heard trash cans being emptied outside, then a hose spraying. Then a truck roaring away.

Lloyd was up and reading the newspaper. He greeted me with his usual, "Well, good afternoon," that covered all rising habits. I fixed coffee and toast and read the San Francisco Chronicle.

"Say, I forgot to tell you," he said, "rumor has it there's an apartment going to be empty just below us. We can look at it this morning. Minnie, who lived there, died a few weeks ago. She lived alone. A very nice woman, but a nut if there ever was one."

I set the paper down.

"You want to move downstairs?"

"Well, to go to that apartment, you don't have the stairs. Besides she has a new rug."

One of Lloyd's recent complaints about his apartment was the wall-to-wall shag carpet. Under his favored chair, it had become shadowed from use. Even after it had been professionally cleaned, the shadow had not come out— or it had only returned. Last year I bought a rug remnant to cover it. He and I set it over the shadow. We backed off and looked at it.

"Margo, if you want my opinion, it looks like the dickens."

End of remnant.

"Let's go," I said, wondering when and if to bring up the other moving project.

Because we knew there were people in the apartment, we rang the door-bell. They were an elderly couple, in retrospect I believe glad to have visitors after having spent so much time alone going through the deceased's apartment. I also was sorry not to have exercised more patience with them on our visit in view of what later happened. We shook hands, and they introduced themselves as Louise and Howard Fuller. I would have guessed in their seventies.

Mr. Fuller told us he was the brother of Minnie who had lived there. "She died of a heart attack," he said. "Just like that," and snapped his fingers. "She was eighty-three."

I warily eyed Lloyd, but he seemed unaffected by the information. He was more interested in the rug and the apartment and was glancing around the room, sizing it up. The rug was the same light beige as in his apartment but because the room was darker, being on the first floor, the rug looked evenly clean or evenly shadowed.

"Don't mind my sister, Minnie. As you see, she was quite a character," Mr. Fuller said as they showed us around. I found it dark and therefore a little depressing, not helped by wine-colored swag drapes and heavy Victorian furniture. And certainly not by the unshaved young man slouched on the couch nursing a can of beer. Mr. Fuller introduced him as his nephew, the son of his deceased brother, without giving his name. Nor did the nephew rise. He raised his can of beer in salutation.

The décor in the apartment belonged to the age of a young girl: pillows in the shape of hearts scattered on the couch where the nephew sat, their innocence providing a droll contrast to his unkemptness; in the bedroom, on the bed over its pink spread, was a large china doll reclining against more heart-shaped pillows, another smiled at us from a pink flowered upholstered chair; one wall in the dining room was filled with framed needle points of a cat, the background pink, and on a table was spread a collection of small storybook dolls (how I remember them) dressed in pastel colors, elegant puffy dresses, coiffed hair—blonds, brunettes, and redheads. Our mother freshened mine up and sent them to me in a box for the children Dev and I would someday have. I was about to make a comment on a painting of a big treasure chest, the chest bound in gold and under it written, "Treasure Chest" that hung on another wall, but the cuckoo clock in the room startled us all by suddenly chirping the time. A tiny bird with a big voice, and it bobbed a few times then disappeared and the door quickly clamped shut on it.

The Fullers told us they had been there over a week sorting out the sister's papers and they were still trying to trace her will, if she even had one. Mr. Fuller thought his sister might have hidden the money. Made a game of it.

"My sister Minnie loved treasure hunts. I don't know why," he said. "You could call it kind of an obsession, but she just loved treasure hunts. She always wanted to give them for birthdays, hers or someone's in the family. Could be what she's done with the money, too. Wouldn't put it past her." He laughed, shook his head puzzled.

Mrs. Fuller said, "I don't think she *had* a will because she didn't like lawyers," and an aside to us, "her second husband was one, and they never got along…"

Mr. Fuller interrupted his wife, "I told Minnie she shouldn't have married him, but the Lord took care of that when he died."

"When did Minnie ever listen to anyone?" said Mrs. Fuller.

Since the Fullers gave no indication of slowing down their conversation that threatened to delve deeper into their lives, I was wondering how to find an excuse to leave. Hinting I edged toward the door. Undaunted Mr. Fuller began talking about his family, their father, who had been the engineer for the roller coaster on the boardwalk in Santa Cruz, then he and his wife interrupting each other in their enthusiasm over the history of the place.

I always loved the thrill of roller coasters and said so, prolonging our exit.

Suddenly Lloyd stretched out his hand, said he enjoyed talking to them and bid them goodbye—the "old days" of business considered concluded without fanfare. An abruptness not unlike him anyway. The Fullers stopped in mid-sentence, mouths open, and though grateful to Lloyd, I was embarrassed. They recovered and invited us to return anytime to see the apartment in case they were interested. Lloyd said thanks and he may do that.

"Wait just a minute," still caught up with family history, Mr. Fuller said, "you'd be interested in this. A history of the boardwalk in one of my sister's drawers in the kitchen. There's a photograph of the roller coaster in it just after it was completed."

"I'll get it," said Mrs. Fuller. "It's in the drawer where she kept her phone book. I just came across it today. What a coincidence to be talking about it now."

In a few moments, Mrs. Fuller came hurrying back.

"I've got the roller coaster information," and she handed it to me, "but see what else I found," she said, waving excitedly a purple envelope in front of Mr. Fuller. She handed it to him, "It was under the roller coaster information. It probably would have just stayed there if you hadn't come," she said to Lloyd and me.

"Oh, my goodness!" he exclaimed. "It's what she used for treasure hunts!" He looked at the front of the envelope. "See, it says *The Hunt*." He set it on a table, patted it for later.

While the Fullers were talking about the purple envelope, I looked at the roller coaster information. A slick, glossy picture of the roller coaster on the front in color, on the back a long description.

"How I loved the one in Santa Cruz," I commented.

"Please keep it," Mrs. Fuller kindly said to me. I folded the page with pleasure and slipped it into the outside zippered part of my purse that I rarely opened and figured a good place to keep for later reading. A perfect fit. If asked to even guess what was on the back of the page, besides the description, I would have been centuries off.

I thanked her. I would read it on my return trip home.

Turning to us, Mr. Fuller said, "That's what Minnie did! She did treasure hunts with colored envelopes so people couldn't miss them. They all had different colors. Good old Minnie, carrying on tradition. She's probably up there laughing. This will be fun. I'll bet she's hidden her life's savings. Yep, as I say, just like her. She never had a will."

At that Lloyd and I found the moment to leave. We both thanked them once more. I glanced at the nephew to say goodbye and found he was already looking at me, the first time he showed any interest in us. But I could have done without that kind of interest, which did not indicate benign thoughts. Not knowing him, I couldn't imagine what kind. Maybe his uncle just ran out of beer.

I wondered if he would be helping them on the treasure hunt.

Opening the door of his apartment, Lloyd said, "That place doesn't compare to ours. There's no light. And you don't get the cathedral ceilings like we have since we're on the second floor. To tell the truth, Margo," he concluded, tossing with great finality his keys on the desk by the front door, "I get exercise by climbing the stairs."

The definition "exercise" was a new one.

"And I've got to say," he went on, "that place is damn depressing."

After lunch I took a walk on the Rio Del Mar beach. I spread out a blanket and opened a can of very cold beer that had been in the fridge during the foggy days waiting for this occasion, a ritual of mine in toasting my return. Having spent childhood vacations here with my mother and father, the sight and smell of this ocean was deeply imbedded in my soul. Today the ocean thrashed, its waves exploding on the shore, salt and the smell of fish mingled, filled the air.

I took a long walk, popped the yellow kelp with my footsteps, and strolled ankle-deep through the icy water until my aching bones couldn't take it anymore. I watched the sandpipers on fast, toothpick legs furiously peck for food at the water's edge, then scamper back at the last second when a wave rolled in. Their built-in radar of clean escapes fascinated me. On family vacations, I would watch them for a long time hoping to catch one less sure-footed. One day I gave up: never caught, they never would be.

Over the high waves, there were pelicans flying and diving for fish; in the distance, gulls flew low-looking—except the ones now making a circle around me for handouts that I did not have.

I wanted to take back with me all of it today. We were soul mates, Lloyd and I, in the sense we both had our memories here in Santa Cruz. Only he had *lived* here for over twenty years. For the first time, I put myself in his place, and in no way would I want to move to Boston, or for that matter in the suburbs of Washington, D.C. I felt somewhat ashamed that Nina and I had been judging his needs based on what we viewed was good for him. But the progression of age has the upper hand. It is so as it is so the sandpipers will always get away.

For dinner I cooked a lamb stew, always on the menu during my visit. Something Lloyd would never make for himself and he loved it, as I did. I was grateful, for he was one with finicky tastes: he liked sugar on his salads, sweet rolls of any kind, always cold, and an expert on their various productions—was not crazy about vegetables and only HE could buy the bread, which he claimed was the best in town (though it crumbled when you put butter on it). On visits it fell to me, or Nina, to throw away food from the freezer he stated had seen its day, claiming he'd never eat it—homemade gifts from friends and therefore he did not have the heart to do the deed himself. I did not delude myself concerning my own dishes that I tenderly prepared while there to freeze, for at times a few of them had turned up on a subsequent visit among the frozen that had "seen its day" when I was performing the weeding out. I was fatalistic.

From where we sat for our meals, we could see the sunset and tonight because the sky was clear, streaks of orange and magenta were vivid. The colors stretched in layered ribbons behind the hills.

Lloyd always refrained from asking me about Dev, and frankly, except for my thoughts about him on this trip, I had moved on. So far I had not been asked about my romantic life—a blunt Lloyd question—but he had not. There was nothing on the horizon anyway, and he probably suspected this. We talked about friends of his and our mother's—the ones here and the ones they left behind in Salt Lake. He told me how good the stew was and accepted the idea of coffee.

By now the sky had darkened and it reached in, touching the chairs in the living room, coloring the walls in shadows. Lloyd pulled out a cigarette, lit up, then rested his arms on the arm-rests of his chair. I walked across the room to the high round table and turned the lamp on.

He tapped the ashes from his cigarette in the ashtray that had *Reno* written on the bottom of it. It was always on the table, there or carried into the kitchen. I wondered about any significance for him, they having married in Reno. Or maybe the importance had been Mother's. Then I would forget to ask.

"I'll put the kettle on," he said, getting up.

I gathered up the dishes, he turned the tea kettle on, pulled two cups from the cupboard, reached in another for the sugar bowl. In it were small packs of Nutra Sweet. He opened one and poured it into his cup. He pulled the box with packs of real sugar from the cupboard and what I took mornings. I put a bit of milk with the sugar in my cup, and we rattled around together in silence for a few moments, each preparing our coffee: kettle sounding, hot water in the cups over instant coffee, and a stir.

"Lloyd," I said out of the blue, "how'd you like to take a trip to Salt Lake?"

"Salt Lake? Where'd you get an idea like that?"

"Oh, I don't know," and didn't. "It just hit me. We could stop in Reno on the way."

"Now wait. Just like that, go to Salt Lake?"

He was standing with the tea pot in his hand. He had his apron on for doing the dishes. It came down to his knees, bright yellow and in black letters across the bib was written "GOOD COOK." It was a Christmas present from Nina.

"We'll buy some nice flowers and put them on Mother's grave."

I dared say that because buried there was also my father, and I suspect why he never returned after her burial. But I did say it. Fact sometimes must be faced.

"I'm not going to the cemetery, Margo, even for your mother. She's with our Good Lord now, and that is it."

"Well, okay. How about the Hotel Utah? You could check it out."

"Say, now you're talking. I heard the place has been redone."

I had taken my coffee into the living room and was sitting on his leather ottoman facing him, drinking his coffee at the dining room table. Even from there I could see his face bright with the mention of the hotel.

"What I'd like to do is go sit there in the lobby and watch the people. I used to do that you know, before I met your mother. Many interesting people pass by. A better show than the movies. Also, a good idea for the car. It needs a long run."

"What about leaving in a few days?"

"I don't see why not. Tomorrow I'll take the car to have the oil and brakes checked."

He went in the kitchen and began loading the dishwasher, rinsing off the dishes that I handed him.

"Lloyd," I said, his back to me, "I think it'll be fun."

"If we don't, it was your idea," he said gruffly. But I could see a lightness in his movements.

2.

NINA AND I ALWAYS INVITED LLOYD'S FRIENDS (AND OUR MOTHER'S) for dinner on our visits. They were five that Lloyd kept in touch with after she passed away, the core and extent of our serious home entertainment. Three of them, ladies, lived in the same condo complex and once in a while invited him for a game of bridge or even dinner. He, a source of needed telephone numbers from his long list, and the three ladies were always grateful.

Occasionally he would make a clean sweep of it and take the three of them to a restaurant. Dinner in his own home was up to Nina and me. All three of the women lived alone. All three of them were in their seventies. Two were sisters. One of them, Junie, used to be a good friend of our mother's—I had not realized how good until I saw her deep sadness when she died.

Junie had married a soldier during the second World War and a few months later was a widow. She never married after that. That history had always struck me as very poignant. Mostly she so young and never marrying again. A love so strong and never found once more. She and her sister, Carol May, came from a genteel southern family. Due to various reasons, and both the sisters being then single, they arrived finally in Santa Cruz and ultimately in the condo complex where our mother and Lloyd lived. They were both vivacious ladies, the quintessential Southern Belle, feminine-looking with fair, curly hair, graceful movements using their hands as they spoke. I loved to hear them talk. They were from Georgia, and voices were as soft as their accent. When I spoke, it sounded hard and brittle against their·words.

Carol May had been divorced for many years. She had heart trouble, and there were times when I felt I could actually see her heart palpitate, lift and fall under her dress when she was having a crisis and where she would take a deep breath and put a hand to her chest, then Junie would quickly reach for her purse, always close to herself, bring forth the pill, give it to Carol May who would swallow it from a shakily held glass, and things would be right again. Used to this, the sisters would take up talk once more as if it had never happened.

Lloyd always commented on Carol May's health after we left them on a visit or after wherever we had seen her, even if there had been no pill scene. His prediction was that Carol May would not last long on this earth, and she was a sick woman.

"She is a very sick woman, Margo. It's a damn shame. She won't get through the year."

I'd known Carol May for over five years and could always count on Lloyd giving his prediction. If Carol May so far had proved him wrong, credit goes to Junie's purse or Carol May's own strong survival instincts. Another suffering was the fact her son lived in Canada, too far for her to visit for health reasons. Her son could not return—at least for some time—due to his avoiding the war in Vietnam when called. He not alone, in Canada, with those beliefs.

Waverly was a New Englander. She was a straight-laced, serious person who had never married. During the war, she was in the WAC's and entertained us with a lot of WAC stories. She drove a Red Cross jeep, and a lot of her stories were of harrowing experiences. Wavey, everyone called her Wavey, was a tall, thin woman, and I could picture her in a jeep sitting tall and straight, maneuvering the steering wheel adroitly over any kind of terrain. She was given a medal—so said one of the sisters—though Wavey never mentioned it.

I sometimes wondered if one of them was interested in Lloyd. He showed no interest in them, and I knew it was not an act for my sake. For one thing, Wavey was too tall for him, and I questioned her interest in men anyway; Carol May too sick, and Junie probably considered herself too·close a friend of our mother to allow herself to have any designs on him. And Lloyd was eighty-three after all. Even if the numerous Cokes he consumed may have played a part in bringing him safely to this age, time sets its rules. Furthermore, if Lloyd were younger, I couldn't imagine him with anyone else besides our mother. They'd had a good one, and as he once said to me, "So be it."

Dorrie and Marshall Whitman were the other two friends. Dorrie a few years older than I. Dorrie used to be Mother's hairdresser but not long ago went into real estate to supplement their income. Marshall taught psychology at a community college but was on leave because the school was low on funds. This was the first marriage for both of them, and they'd only been married a few years. Dorrie had been kind of a substitute daughter for our mother since Nina and I lived so far. They often went to the movies together—Lloyd hated movies, never went after having worked so long in the business. I was not comfortable with Marshall. He was a macho kind of guy, not very interested in what we women had to say, most of all his wife. He was also long-winded, belaboring points, and a good kick in the shins under the table by Dorrie might have put a stop to it. I could not imagine her doing that. Not a strong-willed person, Dorrie would allow him to put her down, contradict her, show impatience with her opinions. Clearly he considered himself a few notches above her intellectually. I liked Dorrie, who deserved more than this husband, for she was bright and funny, but when Marshall was there, always in a temperate way. She was a pretty woman with dark red hair and green eyes, and that alone made me think Marshall was lucky. The pixie haircut fit her bright personality as did the hoop earrings she often wore. But style stopped there, above her neck, with another kind of taste: a sweater with small pink bows printed on it or a full-length skirt that was just slightly too short for her. Her contradictive taste in clothes hinted at a certain vulnerability, an uncertainty in not having quite decided on her kind of role in being a woman. But then I don't know what she thought of me as most the time I wore jeans and a T-shirt.

Conversely Marshall seemed to know who he was, even if he had never been in the military —and I knew through Lloyd he hadn't—for he looked like a member. He was of normal height but seemed taller because he stood ram-rod straight and with his buzz haircut gave the impression he was going to salute any moment. His eyes were a clear, cold blue that rested on others when they talked as a sergeant to subordinates.

Dorrie and Marshall lived in a mobile home. Lloyd has his own opinion about it.

"I wouldn't give two cents for where they live. No better than living in a big bus."

But this was directed more toward Marshall than anything else because Lloyd didn't much care for him either. Mother saw it from another point of view, in trying to be positive for Dorrie's sake, and simply an example of changing a life style. Which was what Dorrie had done after she married Marshall. Before that marriage, she had lived as an earning single woman in a comfortable apartment that had a view of the ocean. This she had given up for marriage and a change of lifestyle. Why, I can't imagine. Our mother never delved into it.

I was not in the mood for someone like Marshall for dinner—ever—and certainly didn't relish seeing one such as vulnerable Dorrie sitting back and taking it. But she obviously loved the guy.

I spent the day cooking, with Dorrie in mind. I felt I had to make up for the bread she cooked for Lloyd that he subsequently left to languish in the freezer (she being one of the poor souls whose efforts were a lost cause). Nothing held even close to his favorite bakery bread, and if Dorrie knew this, she could have bought him a loaf and saved herself cooking trouble. This trip I found it still in the freezer with *Lloyd* written on it and *Love, Dorrie*. I was sorry.

For dinner I prepared a ham with sweet potatoes, then Lloyd and I drove across the street to the grocery store. I always found an excuse to drop by the store on my own. There was a sense of another world about the place. For one it was the quintessential small neighborhood store but different—classy. It had high quality goods, and the floor was wood and creaked pleasantly as you walked along aisles, those stacked with California wines, cheeses, fresh fruit, and the large San Francisco crabs and any other fish one could think of. The butcher, probably as old as Lloyd, had been there for years—experienced and as familiar with a butcher knife as Lloyd with the steering wheel of his car. You asked for an original piece of meat—he could do it. He worked silently, with love in his heart. The clerks knew most of the customers, including me, because they usually stayed put until retirement. They always asked Lloyd about his health, and if someone his age had passed away, they'd tell him, as if that would make him thankful he was still alive.

"Charlie Furman died." Lloyd gave me the information while starting the car. He had been informed of the death while paying for the groceries. "Hell, he was younger than I am! Poor Charlie! I'd heard he'd been sick for quite a while. Now there's one for you. I'm older than he was and hardly been sick a day in my life. You never know what the Good Lord has in store for you."

He'd always been taken by this fact that he'd rarely been sick. He was not proud of it, it puzzled him. Therefore stories like Charlie Furman just added to the puzzle. Yet for me, news such as that brought me to grope for something to say like, "See, Lloyd, how lucky you are." I found myself often trying to pep up his world for him, perhaps because I thought I would need moral support when his age. But for Lloyd, it was wasted for basically he was at peace with his lot.

Lloyd helped me set the table. I came across the China plates with tiny roses on them stored in the back of the cupboard. I decided to use them as a change. Special dishes for special occasions when I was still living at home. Now they were survivors. I found the matching platters, as well as the cups and saucers. This came to mind the candle-lit holiday meals with our father: *this* China gleaming under them over lace tablecloths, the smell of turkey, crystal goblets of wine (that we drank only on those occasions therefore special). Now I was brought back in time. I saw my grandparents at the table, she with her white hair waved at her temples, he beaming, looking forward to the meal, he heavy and ate with joy, Nina next to me, my mother at the end of the table, my father at the other, he with black hair, pale face, handsome, and then his face blurs, becomes Lloyd's, the rest of the company the same, older, and all of us still over the rose patterned china dishes.

"Margo," Lloyd came up behind me, made me almost jump so engrossed had I been with memories, "here are the napkins." He plopped them on the table. "Gee, I think they'll have to be ironed," he said. "What about a candle?"

"Do you have one?" I asked.

He returned from the kitchen with a half-burned fat one.

"Say, we bought this last year, you and I, at your grocery store," I said.

"Oh, did we? I guess we did at that. Used it also when Nina was here to visit."

It was all in the candle, where it burned down one-half each year. With our five dinner guests. I returned to the thought of his moving. To test it. On the trip would be a good time to bring it up. He and I eating somewhere in a nice restaurant, and I could mention how lovely a candle is on a table, for there would surely be one in the Community Place with a dining room, where one could dine under its glow with friends. After dinner play bridge, hear a lecture…

I let my imagination role on and should have stopped and listened to myself.

"Let's use it," I said, placing the candle on the table. "When lit you don't notice the size." An odd comment on my part. On life? Lloyd hadn't noticed.

I pulled out the iron, put a towel on the kitchen counter, and passed it over the napkins. Lloyd settled himself in a chair in the living room, lit a cigarette, and in the other hand a Coke.

The scent of cooking ham drifted through the room; I stopped a moment, went over, and searched through some tapes and came upon Nat King Cole. Our mother liked him, a part of the fifties, a fallow time, a resting period before Vietnam demonstrations and ego searches—the letting-things-all-hang-out way of thinking that grew into the increasingly pounding rock music, its nervousness and indecisiveness, so symbolic of those following years. *Mona Lisa, Mona Lisa*…Nat King Cole's silky voice lifted on the waves of perfume of cooking ham, wafted through the cigarette smoke of Lloyd's, and I remembered pounding that song out on our piano in Salt Lake, listening to it on the car radio. I filled a bowl of peanuts and set them on the coffee table in the living room for our guests.

"Shucks, I haven't heard that song in years, Margo. Who is that, Nat King Cole? Now what made you put it on?"

"Oh, I don't know. It was just there among your tapes."

No need to mention further that it was nice being taken back into that fallow period, remembering the way it was when we were young and oh-so-innocent. One has to look at memories straight in the eyes, I thought, before doing away with them. Squeeze them out, like you do with a rag, before tossing them aside.

I went into the bedroom and changed. It was getting late, and everyone was coming at five. At six we would eat, and at eight they would leave. Early dinner hours seemed not uncommon in California, and I tried to please: drinks at five, dinner at six, and all concluded at eight, in time to catch your favorite program on TV. At first this astonished me. At this time of year in Santa Cruz, it was all over not long after sunset.

The greatest thing you'll *ever learn is just to love and be loved in return...*Nat King Cole's voice trailed off. Those words of truth always touched me. As for myself, I was waiting for that day, but I'd bide my time.

At 5:15 everyone arrived, and we sat around the coffee table eating peanuts while Marshall pulled out the first of his many cigarettes—who smoked more than Lloyd did. Lloyd looked especially nice. He had purchased for himself a new sports jacket made of mohair, colors of soft browns and greens. He had done this while I was preparing dinner, ventured into Santa Cruz alone, which amazed me, the guy who said he never went there anymore, or certainly by himself. I didn't see it until just before the guests arrived.

"What do you think, Margo? I bought it today."

I told him what I thought, that he looked pretty spiffy. I didn't mention Salt Lake but suspected the new jacket and the Hotel Utah lobby was the reason.

"Salt Lake?" Dorrie said as Lloyd filled our glasses. He had just told them.

"We'll stay there a few days, then come back."

I was relieved she had not mentioned our mother and the cemetery for Wavey began talking excitedly about a trip to Hawaii that she had planned to take in September. I was happy for her and glad not to be doing it for it sounded tiring. I liked the idea of traveling in a car, could wear what I wanted, avoid the offerings of the abundant shipboard food that only led to guilt feelings.

Returning to the subject of our car trip, someone knew a hotel in Reno moderately priced, and Lloyd said he would take it upon himself to call. He liked doing those things. He liked calling the airlines, stores—to know if they had certain merchandise he was looking for, and calling restaurants for reservations, short conversations, obtaining information, then hanging up. In the same vein telephone conversations with Nina and myself lasted about two minutes when he would close with it had been good talking to us.

The subject went on to Reno and gambling, the hotels in Las Vegas, gambling, and the shows, Frank Sinatra who was often there. It was six o'clock and time for dinner.

"Heavens, I forgot the bread! It's in the car!" Dorrie said, heading for the door.

"Marshall can get it," I replied and could hear my false note in his not minding.

"Oh, Dorrie, never mind," Lloyd said impatiently, a tone that only I interpreted as not wanting to deal with her bread.

He caught my warning glance.

"Marshall," he corrected himself, "why don't you get it after dinner?"

Marshall hadn't gotten up anyway. He was not one to do bidding on demand by a woman, even if I was co-hostess. And he liked to eat. One thing I did appreciate about Marshall was his appetite because he ate everything and always claimed it was good. Now he was eyeing my food, waiting for us all to settle down.

Wavey turned suddenly to Lloyd, "Have you seen the people in Minnie Watson's apartment? The one below you? You knew Minnie, didn't you?"

"Oh, the woman who just died. A nice lady. We'd just say hello."

"I'm sure Mother knew her better than Lloyd," I said.

Our mother, always friendly, knew almost everyone in the condo buildings.

"Yes, she did," Lloyd said. "She felt sorry for her because she didn't have children. Also, as I recall, she was lame. I don't know if that had anything to do with her peculiar ways of dressing."

At that point, I gave Lloyd credit for not using the word "nut" as he did with me.

"You're talking about her relatives, the ones there now, Wavey? Margo and I were down there just a couple of days ago."

"For goodness sake. Then you did see the people."

"Sure," said Lloyd. "Mr. and Mrs. Fuller. We'd gone to look at the apartment. I'd been thinking of moving there, so I wouldn't have to climb these stairs. Very nice people. Very polite. He was her brother. A nephew there, too."

We talked about them for a few minutes. No one knew there was a nephew. No one had seen him. But then it was concluded that a death usually brought forth relatives previously unknown. Wavey said she had met the brother and his wife some days ago and talked about all the work there was to do in sorting out his sister's things...

"Always so much to do in deaths..."

I added, "One relative had been the engineer for the roller coaster here in Santa Cruz. When they heard on our visit that I was interested, Mrs. Fuller remembered Minnie had some information on it. She found it and was kind enough to let me have it. I'm keeping it in my purse, and when I return home, I think I'll frame it. It's just one page. On the front is a beautiful photo of the roller coaster and on the other side a long description. For me it was always amazingly scary and fun. For most kids, I guess."

The three ladies pulled out some gossip about Minnie.

"She'd been a very attractive woman, you know," said Junie. "She showed me her scrapbook. She was quite proud of it. There were photographs of her when she was young with dark hair and a lovely smile. I don't know where she got her money, do you, Carol May?" her sister asked.

"Oh, she got it through her first husband. From what I heard, he had made it on the stock market. Without children I guess she inherited it all when he died. And it was quite a bit—which was why the second one married her, she told me. I was surprised at how frank she could be. I certainly wouldn't have said that to anyone. She must have been desperate just to marry if she knew all the while he was doing it for her money. Then after all that, the man died."

"Served him right," said Lloyd.

Dorrie and Marshall were quiet. Marshall was quiet because he was eating. Probably grateful the ladies were talking, giving him the chance.

"So the relatives in the apartment must be the ones inheriting her money," Dorrie said.

"Maybe they are, but the brother's wife told me they were sure she didn't have a will," said Wavey.

"Could be she hadn't made one out," I suggested. "The brother told us she hated lawyers. And banks."

"Well, if she didn't, they'd have a long time dealing with the courts," Lloyd said.

"What if she wrote out her own will?" I offered; the subject was becoming interesting to all of us, not less to me, an avid reader of mystery stories, "and then hid it. Her brother said she loved treasure hunts."

I looked over at Marshall. "Is a will valid without a lawyer?" I was sorry I had asked him. Sorry to distract him from his food, and just because he looked like a military man with his buzz haircut, why should he know?

"A lot of times it'll hold up if there's nothing else. One would have to prove she was of sound mind when she wrote it, and for that there would have to be a credible witness."

He broke a piece of bread and spread butter on it. It crumbled as he did it—Lloyd's bread. Undaunted he used the biggest piece of the whole broken thing and continued to butter it. He was careful about it, his hands were clean and white, his nails well-trimmed. He spread the butter evenly on the piece—a tidy person—put the knife down, then bit into the piece. We all found ourselves watching him, waiting for him to continue because he sounded knowledgeable. Along with the fascination of one slabbing butter on a tiny piece of bread.

"But I'm not a lawyer, so don't take my word for it," he said, a note of such derision in his voice when he pronounced the word *lawyer* that I wondered what his experience had been with them. It seemed questionable. It came to me at that moment we never did quite understand what Marshall did for a living. I couldn't imagine him as a teacher, although I don't know why. Because they lived in a trailer, he automatically fell into the category of a laborer, one who worked with his hands, maybe drove trucks, hands used for repairs along the road or handling the provisions he hauled. But cared for as they were, they did not fit into that type of occupation. With our mother, we did not venture into the background of Marshall. He and Dorrie had been married only a short time before she passed away, and because of her affection for Dorrie, she did not want to go into any lurking bad news about her husband. Moreover Lloyd gave her away at their wedding, she without living parents.

I recall once when Lloyd and I questioned with our mother Marshall's occupation and trailer life, she closed the subject saying, "Anyone can live in a trailer. Dorrie's happy, that's what counts."

Dorrie took a sip from her wine glass. "Could be she stashed all her money somewhere. That's not unheard of among older people."

"And lose all the interest?" Marshall said. "Maybe *you'd* do that."

I added quickly, trying to keep my anger in control, "If I were lame and elderly, I might not care much about interest. With probably a lot to live on and it was stored in a convenient place, I'd just go to where I stashed it when I needed some. Sounds good to me, Dorrie. For me it seems that's what she did. When we were there, the Fullers came across a colored envelope while looking for the information on the roller coaster. It was in the same kitchen drawer. Mr. Fuller was pleased because on the front of it was written the word HUNT. He was sure it was the beginning of the hunt for her hidden money.

Because that's what he thought she had done. Hidden all her money. No will. She would leave it that way for her survivors to find. A game. It fit in with her interest in treasure hunts. He said she did it for birthday parties, and in seeing her apartment, decorated with dolls and pinks, the taste of a young girl, one could believe it. She may still have been living in the past. Mr. Fuller said she used different colored envelopes to easily spot in their hiding places. He didn't open the envelope in front of us, but he was obviously excited about the whole search."

What Minnie Watson had done with her money had become an interesting speculation, a good dinner table conversation. It surpassed political talk, Marshall's primary interest and whose discourses led to my indigestion. I could count on being singled out to receive his opinions on world happenings just because I lived in Washington. I welcomed Minnie.

"Hey, let's make this a good one," said Marshall. "How did she die? Say the money was stored somewhere, someone in the family knew where, did away with her and got the money." He laughed. "A good story anyway."

"Only I happen to know she died of a heart attack, at least that is what her brother, Mr. Fuller, told us." I looked over at Lloyd waiting for his confirmation.

"Now wait a minute. Let's stop right here. They were good people. It's all their business. Let's turn the conversation. The whole thing is making me tired. Wills and things. Hell, I'm eighty-three. I don't want to talk about it anymore."

He was the senior citizen at the table and he was right. Often, because he is quiet in a group, the conversation will rise above him, and this time we had all gotten carried away. We changed the subject.

The first to agree with that was Marshall and to give him fair credit for a lop-sided compliment added, "It's your fault, Lloyd, because you don't look eighty-three." He had finished his meal and began an approach on world topics, but by then we were on dessert, sipping the rest of our coffee, and I knew the discussion wouldn't last long.

"Marshall," Lloyd said, "before you leave, please bring in the bread that Dorrie made."

I caught a glimpse of the time and saw it was almost eight o'clock. We were right on schedule.

Junie said, as they all rose from the table, "Instead of Reno, you might consider Truckee, a small town in the Sierras. It should be beautiful this time of year. There's a very nice hotel there. The Fletcher Hotel. It's been around a long time, but I believe they've remodeled it."

"Why not," I said. "I'm game."

"I've been there," said Lloyd, and Junie's right. We could do it instead of Reno. I was in Truckee once on business, way before I met your mother. A very pretty town."

Marshall returned with the bread, Lloyd thanked Dorrie saying it was the best bread he'd ever eaten. Probably the same praise each time she brought a loaf and the great incentive to bake another.

"Sounds like a nice trip," Marshall said. "Good to get away once in a while. Have you set the departure date?"

"In three days, early morning. That okay with you, Margo?"

I agreed and thought it was nice of Marshall to show interest. I gave him a small plus.

It was 8:30 when we bid the final goodbye to our guests. Time for the news.

We spent the next couple of days packing and whatever else one has to do before a trip, including Lloyd calling the hotel that Junie suggested. The day after our dinner, I strolled into town to pick up a couple of books to bring along from one of the three well-stocked bookstores. On my return, crossing in front of the condo building, I couldn't help a sly sizing up of the apartment below Lloyd, wondering if they had finally found the will. All was quiet. The shades were drawn. Had they been drawn before? I couldn't remember. Living on the second floor, as Lloyd did, seemed a good idea just from a point of view that it was private. For that I was glad he decided not to move to Minnie's. I imagined the elderly couple searching, following directions from what was written inside the purple envelope that Mr. Fuller could hardly wait to open and would lead to the next colored envelope. It amused me to think about it then, imagine how much money she could have hidden. That is if Minnie Watson *had* hidden it. I figured she probably had. Maybe I would have done so, too. I tended to be one who could at times procrastinate, especially if it had to do with an expensive lawyer—and if not expensive, I would wonder why he wasn't therefore a no-win situation. Living alone perhaps she had become a little tight-fisted and therefore had taken matters into her own hands and hid the money.

At the bottom of the steps to Lloyd's apartment was a magazine with Minnie Watson's name on it, probably dropped by the mailman. For a moment, I considered ringing the doorbell and giving it to them, I confess an excuse to know if they had found the will. Memories of the nephew and the drawn shades canceled this idea. The little I had seen of him, I continued to wonder about. With all his talk about hippies, I was surprised Lloyd had not vocally put him in that category after we left. I imagine he forgot about him, still thinking about how glad he was he lived where he did. For myself I put him in the *hippie* category. Then with guilt, crossed the thought out because it seemed too often conclusions came to hippie definitions on seeing a person as the nephew. Therefore, to be generous in surmising, I thought of him coming forth with fresh, young, healthy ideas on where to look for the will. Calling out with great politeness and respect those ideas to the Fullers, who were indeed grateful for another opinion. That was believable, just because he could easily perform the task from where he was well ensconced on the couch. Suddenly, as if those thoughts brought him outside the door, the nephew appeared. He smiled and greeted me as I passed by, and I did the same. He was a different nephew, shaved and in good humor. He had a suitcase, and at that moment, a taxi pulled up and the nephew got in and left. I figured they had found the money, given him some and now he was off to enjoy life. A happy conclusion to take with me on the trip. Yet, I wondered why his uncle was not at the door to see him off, correcting myself because goodbyes had probably taken place in the house.

3.

THE MORNING OF THE TRIP WAS FOGGY. LLOYD, ALWAYS POSITIVE regarding fog, assured me it would burn off. Fog did not bother him anyway. He liked it because it was useful as free air conditioning in summers and an excuse to light a fire other times.

I stood at the window drinking my coffee and watched the white mist swirl. This time it had blocked off any view of Santa Cruz and even five feet in front of me where one could barely make out the wood slats of Lloyd's wide deck. It seemed a substance, particles made up of fine bits of sand. I coaxed Lloyd to take his time, thereby giving the weather a chance to clear for our drive along Route One that wound along the scenic ocean coast. In preparing for our departure, I realized how worry-free a condo was, its high windows safe from robbers, no garden to put in order, no threat of bursting pipes. All one had to do was lock the sturdy front door. This conducive in allowing one to become travel-happy. Lloyd brought the car out from the garage, and I made him wait in it, strongly against his will, while I brought down the suitcases.

We would take Route One all the way to San Francisco, then turn inland in the direction of Reno and finally Truckee. Lloyd had made reservations at the hotel in Truckee, and we would arrive there towards the end of the day.

He started the trip choosing to be in the driver's seat. I would have preferred it the other way just because it would condition him to put up with me at the wheel given we were to share the driving. He had taught Nina and me to drive—at the time there was only stick shift. This meant learning to balance the clutch and gas pedal together into a smooth departure.

Now, Margo, what are you doing that for? car lurching forward, my never seeming to get the hang of it.

For Lloyd I would always be the pupil, coupled with the male attitude that men were born as drivers. An exception was allowing me to take the car alone on my visits. But I knew he would be waiting. Last year, on my Santa Cruz visit, I had taken the car as usual to the beach. But on my return, I could not remember where I had parked it. It was a big lot, full and not helped by the car being beige as it seemed most of them. Time passed, I wandered, and all the cars looked beige, and soon dusk would be on its way and fog, and I would never find it. I wandered. I did not have his phone number and I could feel panic growing because he would have no car to come looking for me. He was eighty-two, not a healthy age to be standing at a kitchen window waiting for someone who was not returning *his* car. Suddenly, out of the blue, for no reason I came upon it. It was not the result of looking because, forlorn, I was close to tears. Therefore I knew my mother had a hand in this.

When I returned, I quickly parked the car and ran up the flight of steps. "I'm back!" I called, sounding a bit victorious. He was engrossed in watching a ball game and had not heard me.

As we drove, the fog had begun to lift, and by the time we reached Half Moon Bay, there was a bright haze of sun in the sky. Now I was glad Lloyd was in command, so I could see the views that changed continually: stretches of smooth beaches, the ocean lapping the edges, rocky inlets and further out waves battering the smoothed boulders making them glisten as if oiled. Because it was early spring, the contrast of yellow wild flowers rose high among ragged shrubs and thick tufts of grass. I opened the window a few inches to let in the sound of the ocean, and the air came in briny and moist.

After passing San Francisco exits, we took Highway Eighty, and along the way, we stopped for coffee. Lloyd wanted to drive until Sacramento. I was surprised at his steadiness at the wheel, the sureness in how he handled the highway, even the speed was kept even. He drove as a person much younger than himself or one who had had the experience of driving for so many years. I did not tell him for fear he would insist on driving the whole time.

The highway cut through the fertile Sacramento Valley. On either side, flat land stretched off meeting the horizon, land now blurred green from spring shoots. Lloyd was not one for doing much conversing while driving, probably because he had spent so much time on the road alone. I was able finally to get some reception through the static on the radio and came across a classical music station. I watched the farmland stream by, remembering trips with my mother and father across the land on our way to vacation in Santa Cruz. For as a child, we had lived a number of years in Sacramento. Scenes came to mind now: an eight-year-old hearing classical music played on Sundays in the household, a father in heavy overalls digging in a fenced-in backyard, roller skating on a wide, shiny driveway next door, father, mother, sister sitting around the radio Sunday evenings dining on sandwiches, drinking hot cocoa—because those were the days when the big meal on Sundays was eaten in the afternoon.

Sacramento was where I heard the announcement that the Japanese had bombed Pearl Harbor. Our mother cried.

≈

"Okay, Lloyd, my turn," I said, as we approached the car after having lunched at one of the anonymous highway eateries.

"I'm not tired. I'll drive."

I knew I would have to handle this carefully.

"Why don't I do it for an hour? If it makes you nervous, then you can take over again."

"Well, I don't know. Are you sure you can handle the highway? It's new to you."

"A highway is a highway. How do you think I drive on one when I'm in my own car?"

"Well…"

"Lloyd," I said, becoming assertively impatient.

He handed me the keys.

Within an hour, Lloyd had fallen asleep. That test over, and I concluded successful my attention turned to something else—a car that had been behind us after I had taken over the wheel. It was a dark blue, compact car. I had been careful not to drive faster than Lloyd to keep him from complaining, and as a result, most the other cars were passing us, except the blue one. It had had its chance many times. I chided myself for being suspicious, for why would a car follow us? I felt increasingly uncomfortable. It was impossible to see who was in the car—man or woman—since it seemed on purpose to keep space between us.

Dev came to mind; he was still furious because I left our marriage and now was out to take revenge, or it was his wife who could not stand living with his anger over what I did and it is *she* who is following us. My mind was racing in ridiculous directions. I tried to stop thinking about it and concentrated on driving. I looked over at Lloyd, who continued to sleep peacefully. I should have been glad about his sleeping, now I wasn't so sure. I would have liked to confide in him about the whole thing.

Then he would have said, "Oh, come on, Margo, you're imagining things," and "Dev? Now I've heard everything. That's one for the movies."

He was eighty-three-years-old, even if he were awake, would I tell him about the car that, as I glanced in the mirror, was still following us? If he believed me, it was not a good idea because of his age. If he thought I was imagining things, he might not let me drive anymore. *Sleep, Lloyd*, I thought. Maybe the car is going slow because it's suffering from car trouble. In a while, we'll have to stop for gas and we'll lose it.

At the sign for gas, I pulled off the highway. The maneuver woke Lloyd.

"Where you going, Margo?"

"To get gas."

"What time is it?"

"3:30."

"My gosh. Have I been asleep for an hour and a half?"

"Yes, and we're both still alive."

He laughed. "Well, I taught you to drive. I guess you still remember something from it."

"I'll drive on to Truckee," I said. "Is that alright?"

"Sure. Go ahead."

I was relieved. Being the driver, I could keep my eye out for the car, though it was nowhere in sight while we waited for gas. My uncomfortable feeling subsided and then I felt a bit of shame and how I could imagine such things. Along with locking my mind into memories of the past these days, I was becoming neurotic and suspicious.

With the car full of gas and driving toward the exit that led to the highway, I saw the blue car parked off to the side. I couldn't tell if anyone was behind the wheel, but then that question was answered because it pulled away and eased up at a distance behind us. I turned onto the highway as fast as I could and sped off, causing the tires to screech.

"Margo!"

"Sorry, Lloyd, the gas pedal caught."

"What's the matter with it? I had the car checked before we left. That's a helluva note."

"It's okay. I'm sure it's nothing. Something must have been caught. There it is, a slight rock," I lied. "I just slipped it out with my foot. Probably from the person who had been checking it before we left."

Stupid cover-ups can come to mind to defend lies, and that was one of them. It must have made some kind of sense because Lloyd apparently believed me.

"Go slow," he said, "don't go over sixty-five."

To go faster would not have been a good idea. I could not picture myself in a successful car chase equal to those in the movies. Alone I might have tried it—only with the hope of being stopped by a patrol car, getting help. But there was no patrol car, and I did not want to bring down the ire of Lloyd. Besides no one would believe me if we were stopped, the car would simply disappear. We would go to Truckee at sixty-five miles-an-hour. I tightened my hands on the wheel to keep them from trembling because I was beginning to actually believe it had something to do with Dev. Who else would follow us? What could his/her intention be? I dared not think. Oddly my main emotion for the moment was rage with him. It was *his* fault that I left our marriage. It was *his* fault that all those children were dead, and at that point, I could not allow myself to think any more about it. The radio suddenly became full of static. and Lloyd switched it off.

"Margo," he said, "what would you think if Junie moved in with me?"

Juxtaposed to the blue car in the rearview mirror were the words of Lloyd, with it came the statement that God gives us only what we can handle.

"If Junie moves in with you?"

"I didn't know how to approach it. I wanted to tell you earlier, then you came up with the idea of going to Salt Lake, and I thought that would have been as good a time as any. Junie's a fine woman. Both of us are alone. With your mother…that can never be replaced. I'm sure you know that."

Junie? Junie and Lloyd? My mind closed in on it. For a wild moment, I forgot the car. She had been a good friend of our mother's. I liked her. Images and thoughts raced through my head. I couldn't picture Lloyd with someone else. He was a loner, that was his identity, he was there waiting for us to come visit, for his coming to us at Christmas, he had needs that had to be taken care of by Nina and myself, he was Lloyd, alone and widower of our mother, now old by himself, and that was the way it would always be. I could not imagine this in any other state. I was glad I was driving. He had actually picked a good time, and I could stare at the highway and gather my thoughts.

"I…heavens, I don't know what to say, Lloyd. I hadn't any idea…You mean you want to *live* together, you and Junie?"

I was fumbling for words, but nothing came except, "You and Junie." I had instant pictures, slides flickering on and off a screen, of Lloyd and Junie doing the housework (she letting his power vacuum lead her around), cooking meals together, she driving to the store across the street with him, wearing the yellow Christmas gift marked, GOOD COOK, getting dressed up and then going out together. Together? Sleeping—*together?* I had an instant picture of that, too, while staring at the highway, Junie and Lloyd in the king-sized bed under the king-sized heating blanket. Better not try to figure anything out.

As for Lloyd bringing it up now, in the car, he had found his moment when I had not found mine about his moving. When and how does one bring forth questions of this sort? What would be the comfort-zone situation where one could bring up the question of a life's change? On the way to Truckee maybe. When one was not aware of a car following us.

He and Junie were left for us to talk about. I am not sure I had really convinced him that I was for it, though I wasn't against it and again told him so. Yet I sensed I had failed him. I had shown no enthusiasm. I had allowed the subject to trail off with his words; we could talk about it during the trip. There was no way for him to know I could not divide my mind at the moment between danger and a proper answer to his question. Yes, it would have to wait, and I was sorry.

With that we changed the subject. To keep myself distracted from the car behind us, I relied on his Chicago days. I hoped my interest would please him, make up for my failure of enthusiasm about Junie. But soon he will know why. We could not go on forever with a car trailing us, and I would have to tell him.

"…we had a lot of fun those days in Chicago, I can tell you. Good, clean fun. Good, clean fun compared to now, drugs all over the place. Sure there was prohibition, and that caused a lot of illegal drinking, but there wasn't the drug problem. The people I knew, well, we all liked to go out dancing. There were a lot of ballrooms then. Fancy, and they'd also serve dinner. Maybe we'd have a drink or two, maybe not. Was a time when everyone got gussied up— now people don't seem to care much. Men wore hats then. Ladies wore hats."

"What about the spats, Lloyd? Tell me about the spats again."

"Well, it was a heavy piece of cloth that slipped over the top of the shoe and around the ankle. Gosh, I haven't thought of them for a long time. They were white and black. I had a damn nice pair, and one of my canes had a sterling silver handle. We wore top hats. Shucks, it was another era, Margo."

"Where did all the single people stay in those days?"

"We lived in the hotel rooms. Some stayed in rooming houses. Most the people I knew lived in hotel rooms—even married ones if they couldn't afford a home. We'd take our meals in the hotel most the time. To live in a hotel room then wasn't so expensive. We didn't have to worry about laundry and we didn't have to cook. Shucks, even that's changed now. I'd be willing to wager that it's been a long time since somebody has lived at The Hotel Utah. They stay a few days, pay their bucks, then go off to the airport."

The Hotel Utah. I had forgotten all about our destination. Uppermost in my mind was Truckee and the hotel—safety. I tried to make out who was driving the car, if there were others in it, but it kept its distance, most the time with another between us. It was not possible to read the license plate, and if I could, it would have been backwards in the mirror. I decided to speed up for a moment just to see what would happen. Lloyd was talking, he wouldn't notice. I slowly raised the speed to almost seventy-five, passing a few cars as I did. The blue car disappeared but shortly reappeared again behind another.

There was no way I was going to shake it. Whoever was driving was very competent. My heart was pounding. I tried taking a deep breath to calm me. Who could I signal? Impossible to believe but no one. There were cars streaming by us, we were surrounded by people but no way to signal for help. Yet what would I say, even if I wanted to? Could I say that somebody was following us while meantime that somebody was not there?

"Margo, did you hear what I said?"

"Oh, I'm sorry, Lloyd, what?"

"When you get a moment, pull over on the shoulder. I want to check the aerial. I think it's not up all the way. That's why the static came on."

"Let's wait about the radio, Lloyd. It's too much trouble to stop. Let's just wait until we get to Truckee."

"It's okay by me. I was just thinking of you."

The idea of stopping scared the wits out of me because the driver of the car might have a gun. Once stopped we were helpless. No, the idea was to keep moving, and I was thankful we had not long ago filled the tank with gas.

"You're a good entertainer, Lloyd. Tell me about Truckee when you were there. We must have about less than an hour to go."

We were climbing now. The wide highway cut through the mountains, the sheer slopes bordering the road a mixture of boulders and tall stately firs, among them were the same yellow wildflowers that I had admired above the ocean shores.

"Truckee used to be a railroad town. The name is from the river called Truckee River. The train passed through it with lumber," he told me once more. We had gone through all this before we left, and he had been enthused about spending the night in the town. Lloyd had been to Truckee various times when in the vicinity on business. "After your mother and I were married and we took the train from Reno to San Francisco, it stopped here in the station of Truckee. You probably don't remember that."

I would have given anything now to have been on a train, not to be on a highway with fear in my heart. I prayed against a flat tire or any other reason that would force us to stop.

It was close to five o'clock, the sun filtered a deep yellow through the tips of the fir trees. Once in a while signs popped up to beware of deer, sliding rocks and icy roads where finally the welcome sign that indicated we were in

Truckee city limits. We edged slowly toward the center of town, following the instructions the hotel gave Lloyd.

"Go slow, Margo. It's on Jackson Street. Right off Maine. We're on Maine, so let's watch for it."

Maine Street was a street lined with brick and shingled buildings: banks, restaurants, a Woolworth's, and other buildings that made up a town, but my mind was whirling with so much confusion that all was a blur, meaningless. I wondered if we should find a police station, but I did not want to begin looking for one, at least until we got inside the refuge of the hotel. I saw in the mirror the car had turned off into Truckee also, it was now some cars behind us, perhaps waiting to see where we would stop. The police station came to mind again, for there must be one, but where? Once more who would believe me at the police station? Lloyd would think I had imagined the car, too, and I wouldn't blame him.

"Where are you going, Margo? You went right by the street. That's Jackson back there."

I turned us around. We pulled up in front of the hotel and Lloyd got out; I glanced back down the street, and with relief, saw it was empty. No blue car.

"You wait here, Margo. I'll go in. I'll send someone out for the bags."

Still nervous I diverted my attention to the hotel, noticing the building for the first time. It was pure ornamented Victorian. I could not imagine how many were the varieties of wood used on the structure. Roof, gables, towers, window frames, balconies, all contrasted in light to dark wood colors but in a soft not garish way. The effect was to make one want to stand back and memorize, take it all in as one would do a scene of nature, a sunset, sea coves, so as not to forget. Curious to see the inside, I decided to go in without waiting.

The interior of the hotel glowed in polished wood, a wide staircase opposite the entrance welcomed guests and wound gracefully up and disappeared, its banisters polished so they seemed mirrors, the dowels intricately carved. The window panes in the large room were all of stained glass, lovely soft pastel colors. It was the light filtering through the rich colors that gave the interior its final glow, greens and reds, deep golds, all settled over strewn flowered carpets and waxed floors; a tall walnut clock in a corner with its deep ticking filled the quiet entrance.

When I returned to the car, I saw the blue one again at the end of the street. It was facing the intersection—an easy way to leave if necessary. The person in the car was obviously watching me from the rear-view mirror. Suddenly it pulled away and disappeared. I opened the car window and took a few deep breathes, the air was pure and cold and calming. Mountain air. Something had to be done. I could not go on like this alone. I would go to the police after settled in my room. The idea allowed a slight feeling of calm. I left the car parked in front and entered the hotel where Lloyd was at the desk talking to the desk clerk. As I approached, I heard the man say he was the owner. Blunt as always, Lloyd responded that he didn't know the hotel existed, even though he had often stayed in Truckee. I covered by reminding him that he probably stayed on the edge of town, and he agreed that was most likely the case. Knowing what might follow would be the question of the location of the Coke machine I quickly said something about the mountain air, how refreshing it was after breathing heavy fog in Santa Cruz. The owner, a kindly older man, healthy, athletic-looking, fitting the sporty category of one in charge of a mountain hotel, said the air kept one young here.

"One comes, one finds it hard to leave."

But under my circumstances the remark sounded only ominous. We talked about the ocean and Santa Cruz, I commented with great sincerity on the beauty of his hotel. The first owner had been a retired sea captain, he said

"I guess he wanted to get away from it all, come here above sea level. And of course it certainly is that. This was about a hundred years ago. He had the house custom built. Seems his wife had a lot to say in that. Then it passed through a few more hands, and my wife and I bought it over twenty years ago.

"There were a lot of repairs to be made, and while we were doing this, we made the decision to turn it into a hotel. Truckee's one of the doors to the Sierra. In the summer, we get a lot of people. Winter, slightly less. They go on up to Tahoe and the ski resorts."

He stretched out his hand to us, "My name's Nelson. Hank Nelson. Please call me Hank. Anything I can do for you to make you comfortable let me know."

He smiled at us over his glasses that were set in the middle of his nose and handed us the keys. I knew I would be down shortly to ask him the first question about the police station.

"Damn, I forgot to ask him if they had a machine here," Lloyd said on the way to the elevator, settled inconspicuously under the staircase.

"Lloyd, they probably don't. We'll buy a case," my knowing that he did not care if they were room temperature.

"Now that's a good idea. In the meantime, you go on up and get settled in your room. I'll have the suitcases brought up and move the car."

I felt cold fear.

"Oh, Lloyd, I'll do it." Although my going out to do it was no less dangerous. "Give me the keys, Margo. I'll be back in a minute."

I handed him the keys.

After getting settled in my room, its four-poster bed under dark, carved wood beams and windows of pale-yellow stained-glass depicting musicians, I set out for the desk again. Lloyd had returned in one piece from moving the car, and I told him I was going to buy him a case of Cokes and look around town. He told me to go ahead. Too far to walk, he gave me the car keys. He had found a newspaper stand next to the hotel and was going to sit in his room and read the local paper, *The Reno Gazette*.

"I'll be finished in about five minutes," he said, referring to *The Gazette*. "It was a bad paper years ago and it probably still is," and the statement amused me in spite of my reason for the police station. The fact was Lloyd went through each of his newspapers in five minutes, be it *The New York Times*, that he subscribed to as well as *The San Francisco Chronicle*. Usually by nine o'clock in the morning, all the papers were stacked neatly, put in their place by the front door ready to throw out. During my visits, I had to guard articles I wanted to read later by hiding those sections under the couch. He found them once and figured they were old papers put by the two women who cleaned. In time I rescued them.

Hank Nelson was still at the desk, and he looked up and smiled as I approached.

"Everything alright?"

"It's wonderful. Your hotel is very lovely, Mr. Nelson." While looking around with true admiration at the beautiful room, I mentioned that my father left his driver's license at home. Perhaps something temporary could be done about it here so he could drive. A police station could advise me.

It was the best excuse I could do without widening what was not yet a problem. A risk with hopes *The Reno Gazette* would hold his interest for a while.

"It's not police here, it's the sheriff's office. His name is Montana. Sheriff Mike Montana. We're a small town, so don't expect too much. But if anyone can do something for you, it's Mike. He's been here all his life. It's only three blocks away. Turn left when you are outside of the hotel, go down a block to Main Street, and turn left again. Walk a block and you'll see it, across the street on the right. There's a flag in front. One thing for sure is you can't get lost in this town. Wait just a minute. I'd better call and see if he's here. He keeps office hours only a few days a week."

Hank picked up the phone and dialed. My heart fell. I was never lucky about those available when I needed something. If the sheriff wasn't there, what would be the next step? Leave tomorrow and pray not to see the car behind us again? By that time, Lloyd would have to know and a whole new worry.

"Mike? Hank." My spirits rose. "I've got someone here who wants to see you. Her name is"—he looked up at me, I whispered Margo Heston. He repeated it to Sherriff Montana.

"She's leaving now," he looked at me questioningly to confirm, and I nodded. He went on to talk to the sheriff of other things, and I made the gesture I was leaving. I had had the ridiculous idea of asking about a taxi since I was not keen on walking alone, but there was no way I could do that and sound sane.

Outside It was still daylight but enough walkers on the sidewalk that helped me blend. A comfort, for I felt a growing fear from being alone. More, would the sheriff still be there? He could not wait? After the warm hotel, the cold air pressed against my light-weight jacket. It was the only wrap I had brought for Santa Cruz, never needing more at this time of year. I was not prepared, and the knowledge that I was headed for a sheriff's office underlined this as another unexpected fact.

The Sierra rose tall behind the town. One special part of it higher, more majestic, a protector— a duty of the powerful—and the purity of its winter-white took over the sky, claimed it, dominated the town of Truckee while its whiteness lengthened on to Tahoe. Loyal, closing us all in her heart as she traveled. The Sierra Nevada.

I learned of her from having looked up the town of Truckee before our trip. Read of the greatness of the range, harboring parks, as Yosemite, owning and sharing the spectacular beauties of the four seasons, as well a home for the living souls She nurtured. Yes, I thought now as I walked, it has forever been so. She a holder of a past with no beginning, of a heartbeat that is vibrant and strong. Yet in seeing her, those see only what is solid, not living, us admirers of her beauty, without realizing that she is a soul bearer.

Soon I came to Main Street, in the distance, on the left I saw the flag as Hank had indicated. I turned. It was then I realized the walkers had dispersed. Then in pure terror, I knew that on foot, behind me, was the driver of the blue car. With the flag in sight, I ran. A car honked, and I ran—up the steps of the building I ran and under the red flag and through opened door where I was firmly stopped by Sheriff Montana.

"Whoa, it's okay. Come, sit down. Catch your breath."

I felt guided to a chair, and he held it out. I sat down but could not stop trembling. He was standing quiet in front of me, I saw only his legs as I was bent over hugging my crossed arms. I tried not to cry from this sudden kindness. *Big girls don't cry…Big girls don't cry…*an echo from somewhere.

"You're shaking. I'll turn the heater on. It gets cold pretty fast without it. I just turned it off and was going to leave when I was told you were coming. Glad I was still here. I'll brew some coffee, then you can tell me about it."

I hadn't been prepared for his immediate understanding. For I had interrupted plans he probably had after leaving. But then I forgot I was out West where friendliness prevailed, especially in small towns. Nor was I prepared for Sheriff Montana himself. I had imagined an elderly man, or at least older than Montana, one who fit Mr. Nelson's description of having lived in town all his life. A life that I assumed had been a long one.

He was tall and slim, skin pale, Indian blood showing only in his black eyes that were long and narrow and fit his graceful form, blending in the way that Nature balances. This I took in as I watched him calmly prepare a cup of coffee for me on his desk. Done silently, allowing the calm in the room to take over quietly. To slow a heart rate, that had kept me from words. My own words.

I had a picture of myself. The little attention I had been giving to it after I left our marriage—knowing and doing nothing about it. Moreover Lloyd was one who, if took notice, drew the line at his being over-honest and was too polite to comment. Lately there had been little incentive to think of myself as doing more than necessary. And now, in that moment, I was suffering for it– a fact that brought my suspicion he would not believe me: off the street, a bit flaky. But my heart had quieted. I was safe

Not wanting to disturb him longer than necessary, I pushed vain thoughts from my mind in recalling why I was at a sheriff's office. I knew I should not lose that thread to give me the confidence needed in recounting this to him. To somehow show him I was a normal person. Having reason to be where I am right now, which is Lloyd's and my well-being. Yes, that is true, I told myself, but there will be questions not answerable. I am without a witness.

"I'm sorry, keeping you like this," I began—from one soon to be defined, to fit the definition, as a problem without a witness.

"Don't think about that," he said. "I'm glad I was still here."

"I told Mr. Nelson, Hank, at the hotel it was about my father's—my step-father's driver's license. That was not true."

I laughed self-consciously, "Now at a sheriff's office, I'm between feeling ridiculous and frightened." I stopped to find a meaningful way to present the reason why I *was* there.

"I think we're being followed," I said.

With those words came relief. To have finally shared it. I prepared for some gesture that could reveal he *did* think me odd. I had come to him from nowhere. Before him sat a stranger in town. One who was hysterical.

Without commenting he sat down behind his desk, a movement showing he was ready to hear me out. Perhaps this was the result of being used to listening to many mundane problems that exist in a small town, or a woman with a vivid imagination, thus patience, and it will soon be over. Even so I appreciated his show of interest. There are those who make no pretense at all when covering boredom.

I began from our leaving Santa Cruz bound for Salt Lake, my noticing a car in the distance, always there after I had taken the wheel. I told him how the car had also stopped where we had parked for lunch and it was at the exit when we pulled off onto the highway, following us once more, turning off when we took the exit to Truckee. Lloyd, my step-father, was not aware of it when he drove. I chose not to tell him, not wanting to upset him at his age.

The warmth from the heater slowly filled the room.

He had been watching me without emotion as I talked, eyes black, steady, scrutinizing if they wanted to be but now neutral, not mocking nor showing sympathy. I finished.

He got up, walked from behind his desk, and poured some coffee for me. I watched him silently, waiting for him to finish, watching his movements that were unhurried and thoughtful; he was wearing jeans, a heavy white sweater that contrasted with his black hair that fell in soft strands over the back of the collar.

I looked away quickly, afraid he would turn and find me staring.

"You have no idea if the car was there behind you when you left Santa Cruz?" he asked, gently setting a large mug between my hands. "Here," he said, "let me show you something. Cups this size in Truckee have a double purpose, or at least in my cold office they do."

He took the mug back. "A good hand warmer if the coffee's real hot. Spread your fingers around it, like this," he spread his fingers, long and slender, around the cup, then gave it back to me, sat down at his desk again.

I smiled appreciatively and held it between my hands. There are simple memories that can remain in life, and mine was the warmth that flowed from the cup, filled my hands like a warming sun, and calmed my soul.

In answer to his question, I said, "The car could have been behind us when we left, but there were many cars on the highway, and I wasn't driving, my step-father was."

"And your step-father didn't notice anything unusual then or on the trip?"

"He would have said something, and I didn't want to bring it up. We shared the driving, and I figured it was safer if he did not know. He's eighty-three. There was nothing he could do about it. I didn't want to worry him."

"That I can understand. And you can't think of any reason why anyone would want to follow you?"

"I can't think of anyone," I said. I did not want to mention my suspicion about it being Dev as it sounded pretty ridiculous. "I understand this is hard to believe. Looking back, if I had told Lloyd, my step-father, I would have had a witness. I'm afraid without one this can be taken as my imagination."

"I'm sure you didn't imagine it. It's just the whole thing sounds odd. Don't get me wrong. Odd happenings as this can have a logical explanation. I know you're worried and have a reason to be. Only now it's probably a good idea to mention it to your step-father. At least you might know if he had noticed something about the car when you left. Even if he hadn't given it enough importance to mention it to you."

I raised the mug and sipped the coffee. It was strong but good.

"License number? A long shot, I know."

"No, I didn't get it," I said miserably. "I would have had to ask my step-father for it while we drove, but then I didn't want to tell him about it. But the car was never that close anyway—whoever it was had been careful enough to keep a distance."

He put his elbow on the desk, rested his cheek heavily on his fist, readying himself for a few more tired questions to placate me.

"Can you think of anything that happened to you or your step-father before you left? Something that might not have mattered then but could be related now to a reason someone might want to follow you? Anything at all?"

I drank again from the cup, the steam still rising from it. The fact was I could only think of Dev as the driver of the car, an anger in trying to get even, and I still knew better than to mention it.

"Well, my step-father and I went to the store, we went to the bank, I made some trips alone into town, Santa Cruz...Nothing happened then, we had his friends for dinner, something I do every time I visit. No, nothing," I concluded, "nothing comes to mind that could have been unusual."

"How long are you going to be here, in Truckee?"

"This was to be an overnight stop on our way to Salt Lake."

"It's supposed to snow tonight and maybe continue on tomorrow," he said. "I'm sorry to give you that information."

"Snow? That idea never occurred to us stopping here. It's spring!"

"In the Sierra, it can snow even in June. We had a good snowstorm in June a few years ago. Unfortunately it wasn't earlier to help the ski season because by then the lifts were closed." He laughed, good-humored resignation in his voice. "The Sierra likes to pull fast ones sometimes. She likes to remind us who is the boss. Though for all of us who live here, this is never doubted. Look," he continued, "I'll drive you back to the hotel. If you see the car on the way parked, I'll get the license and we'll work from there. One other thing. Do you know by any chance the make of the car?"

"No," I said ashamed. I looked up at him, "I'm sorry." I felt he was making an effort to believe me—or at least to make me think he did for even sheriffs must please the public. "I've never been good at recognizing the makes of cars. It was compact and a recognizable blue in color, that's all I remember. But then it always kept its distance, enough so that even being an expert I might not have been able to tell."

"That's good enough. Not too many of those in a small town. At least for now. Most of the vehicles here are jeeps or newer cars with a four-wheel drive that probably your blue compact doesn't have. Maybe later you will laugh about all of this. And I agree with you, might be better not to mention it to your step-father, unless of course the car turns up again. In all probability, the car's gone, especially if aware it'll snow around here tonight."

"Are your weather prediction accurate?" I asked worriedly. "I'm sure our car doesn't even have snow tires. They'd be useless in Santa Cruz."

"I'm afraid so. But they usually get the roads cleared fast, and while you're waiting, you can have chains put on and drive to Tahoe to see the lake. And if you like to gamble, there's plenty of that."

"I'm not very lucky when it comes to gambling," I laughed.

"That makes two of us."

He pulled a beige sheepskin jacket off a hook on the wall and slipped it on. Bent down, working on the zipper, he said, "Zippers. They have their own way in this world. I always wondered who invented them."

Jacket closed he looked up. "Let's go." He reached over to the wall hook and took off a brimmed hat, set it on his head. "I hope" he said, "at eighty-three I'll be able to drive from Santa Cruz to Salt Lake City."

But for now, it was Sheriff Montana, far from the age of eighty-three, sheriff of a small town in the mountains, tall, looking in charge with his sheepskin jacket, a wide-brimmed hat on his head, now with the responsibility of a stranger, one who had to force away an attraction to him.

"Perhaps it's the Coke he drinks," I said jesting, bringing some relief. He's addicted to them. Is there a small store by you that sells Cokes? I could run in for a moment and pick up a case. Would you mind too much?"

"Better than that, I have a case in the back room. But they're not cold. I forgot to put them in the fridge."

"He's not particular," I said.

While waiting for him, I noticed a photo on his desk. A young girl, pretty, probably in her teens. He came back too soon for me to look away.

"That's my daughter. She's eighteen now. It was taken a few years ago."

"She looks like you," I said.

"People say that. I think parents are the last to notice. Here's a case of

Cokes. They've been sitting around waiting for the hot weather, and I'm happy to make a gift of welcome to your step-father."

"He'll be grateful. I am, too. I had planned to stop at a store after I left here."

"That's something I wanted to mention to you. Until this is figured out about being followed, don't go out by foot. I would imagine, if the person is still around, he or she has put the car in a garage and in that case mingling with the public. It's okay. Don't worry," he reached out and touched my arm. "You did the right thing by coming here as soon as you arrived. Just be aware when you leave Truckee that you are not followed by a blue car. It'll give you time to turn back to come here." He touched my arm again, "So let's go, and I'll give you a quick tour of the town."

Outside the temperature had dropped some degrees in just the small amount of time I had been in the sheriff's office.

"What you need here is a big down jacket," he said, glancing at my jean-jacket that I liked, that at one time I thought of as stylish and now was only cold.

"To be honest," I said, "I never imagined myself in Truckee these days. Nor in any kind of cold weather. This trip was a kind of a spur of the moment idea."

"What interested you to stop in Truckee?"

"Friends recommended the hotel."

"Did they?" He was locking the door to the office and turned to look at me genuinely pleased. "Every small town likes to have news it's well-known for something. We have a lot of competition here in winter. Most people want to stay in the Tahoe area, go up to ski and then down to the hotels to gamble away all their money. For us in Truckee, tourist season is late June through summer. The wildflowers come out, the trees turn a real chartreuse color and—here I am sounding like a vacation ad. My car's parked in front. No walking. A jeep like the rest of them. None of us are very original in Truckee."

We made a quick tour of the town, and since it was growing dark and there was no sign of the car, he drove me back to the hotel. We had talked little; I was feeling increasingly more foolish not being able to back up any of my story, and he most assuredly wanted to go home. I allowed myself to wonder what his wife was like, assuming he had one, imagined dinner cooking in a warm house. I felt lost in this town that had no meaning, not dressed for it, looking for something that for the time being had not turned up, and moreover, it was going to snow. *Where would we eat tonight?* I thought. It was not good to prowl around in the car with Lloyd because I had the nagging sensation that the car was out there somewhere. And Lloyd would want to prowl around for a place to eat, and why not, he as hungry as I. I would have to tell him about the car and the sheriff's office when I returned because now it was not right to keep silent. I dreaded it.

As we approached the hotel, Sheriff Montana said, reading my mind, "Hank Nelson's wife is a darn good cook. A little secret: if you ask her and when the hotel isn't full, she'll offer the guests dinner in the hotel. You might ask her. You must be hungry and considering you can't go out…"

He looked over at me and smiled. Even in the shadows of dusk, his eyes were a strong black.

"Thanks," I said. "I will do that. You read my mind. I wasn't enthused about going out tonight because of the snow but not possible anyway due to it not safe."

He stopped in front of the hotel, pulled a pen from inside his jacket, and tore off a piece of paper from a clutter of things on the dashboard. "I'm leaving my home number for you just in case, since tomorrow isn't my day to be in the sheriff's office. Call me if you need something. And I wish you both a good trip."

He touched his hat that now threw his face into shadow. I thanked him and got out.

"Your Cokes…don't forget them," handing me the case as I got out. "Caps are screw-on."

"He'd be grateful for either," I said.

He waited until I had arrived at the door of the hotel before pulling away.

A few snowflakes had begun to fall. They drifted lazily through the golden air from the hotel windows, not quite sure where to land, not quite sure even if they should accumulate and become a storm. Maybe it would be they would defy the forecast, tire of indecision and pull back.

I saw Hank Nelson wasn't at the desk and concluded the woman tending it was probably his wife. She was a plump woman, as hardy-looking as her husband, and seeing me gave a friendly smile.

"My husband told me you were looking for the sheriff's office about your father's driver's license. Did you find the office without a problem?"

I thanked her and said I had.

"Sheriff Montana mentioned you sometimes prepare dinner for hotel guests," I added, trying to keep hope out of my voice, the alternative not eating at all rather than risk the danger of being seen on streets by foot. Moreover Lloyd was a slow walker not used to going anywhere without a car.

"Well now," she laughed with good humor, "he told you that? It's not often, but I sometimes do it. It depends sometimes on the weather and if there are few guests."

"He also said you are a very good cook."

"He's my biggest fan. He eats here frequently."

This information I stored in my mind. One who ate out frequently did not eat often at home. I wondered what it meant and dismissed the thought. I was ashamed of being attracted to a person whom I didn't know anything about and furthermore would never see again.

"We're having lamb stew tonight. I'd be more than pleased to serve you in the breakfast room. We have no guests right now, and Mike probably told you we make exceptions then."

She was a pretty woman with large blue eyes and was dressed for the mountains in a dark green knit sweater, a large, white reindeer on the front of it. ·

We agreed on 6:30, an hour away, and I went up to Lloyd's room.

"Well, did you have a good walk?"

The newspaper was neatly assembled near the door ready to be done away with.

"It's snowing, Lloyd, and we're going to eat right here in the hotel. Mr. Nelson's wife offered to serve us dinner in the breakfast room. Lamb stew. How about that? Your lucky night. We eat at 6:30. And here's a case of Cokes I found on the way back. Also, it's supposed to snow tomorrow, too."

"Lamb stew?" His eyes went bright on that note. "Good. Snow in spring? Now who would have thought of that? Well, if it snows, it snows. In a couple of hours, we'll be out of it—and I'll drive—then we'll be in the desert."

I pictured us forging through a snowstorm, an eighty-three-year-old man at the wheel and maybe a blue compact car again behind us. Tomorrow. For now I didn't want to think about it.

When I returned to my room, there was a knock on the door. It was Lloyd.

"Just want to thank you for the Cokes. I'll call for you at 6:30."

I smiled to myself after I closed the door. Lloyd would never give in to sentimental feelings. He knew if he did, we would both be uncomfortable.

I went to my bathroom to freshen up. But before doing that, I stood in front of the wide mirror, part of the Victorian décor in the bedroom. The dark, curled frame, so heavy in its style, was not flattering to my face. Or to any face, I told myself as a kind of pep-talk.

My blond hair, that I usually kept short, hung to my shoulders lank around my face; my eyes, a dark blue—a color that Dev teasingly told me he married me for—reflected how dull and tired I felt, certainly lacking the light in them that Lloyd had when he heard about the lamb stew. Had I always looked this colorless, I wondered. Everything matched in their paleness; it was as if my face, my features, were fading. Queer things happened when the mind was troubled. In my case, features were slowly being sucked away, as night pulls the last rays from the sky leaving it bland and even-looking, and one day they, or the soul, would be completely dry, no identity. I would be nameless. I could not have done it differently with Dev in leaving him, but had I not known about those children killed, I would still be married, happy with a man I believed was a moral human being. This would always haunt me: dice thrown that evening after the movie and what came up was the bar and Dev running into his friend. "Life can turn on a dime"—Lloyd's words. I thought of my attraction to Sheriff Montana and realized it was the first healthy sign of liberation from all the feelings that went into leaving a marriage. But to be honest with myself, I had not met anyone with the power of attraction that Sheriff Montana had.

Dismayed by my appearance, I gathered my hair and pinned it up in the back. *Oh, foolish, foolish lady, for what reason*, I thought as I did it. Where was my eye liner, I wondered. Did I bring it? No, for I was only traveling with Lloyd who didn't care. *Oh, silly lady*, I thought as I rummaged through my purse, remembering I kept one there for emergencies, put there some time ago in the zip pocket. I found it and lined the lower part of my eyes. I put lipstick on, appalled I had not even been using IT these days. The substitute was Chapstick. How had I looked when Lloyd's friends came to dinner? *Washed out*, I thought, like a single woman young enough to start a new life but had not a clue how to do it. Had they guessed? Someone had only remarked that I was thin. Meaning: "Woman, you look pale, featureless, close to losing your identit…"

I had been talking to myself too long in front of the mirror, time enough for self-pity. I loosened strands of hair, so they fell softly along my temples, softened the pulled-back hair-do. I dared not a give a last look before leaving the Victorian mirror—too risky, I'd live with it.

"Say, don't you look snazzy," Lloyd said when he came to call for me on the dot of 6:30.

4.

THE DINNER WAS AS GOOD AS SHERIFF MONTANA PREDICTED.
Next to Lloyd's plate was a tall glass of Coca-Cola, and how they knew about Lloyd's affinity for it, I could not guess. But then I could. After dropping me off, he had the time to pick up the phone and inform them. Moreover there was a fire briskly going in the large stone fireplace. It burned and crackled, sending a cozy warmth through the room, and I had wine that completed the sensation of well-being. Self-pity took wings.

During the meal, Hank Nelson came over and talked with us. We were the only ones in the dining room though another couple, they told us, had checked in while we were in our room. I was thankful that if snow arrived, it was now, not during our drive today through the mountains. Hank discovered Lloyd liked to play poker—another of Lloyd's pastimes when he was a bachelor at The Hotel Utah.

He had asked Lloyd outright about the poker, before he knew Lloyd played because, he said, "I know a card player when I see one." Hank's wife was a poker addict also, and during the slow season, both were always on the lookout for guests who played.

Lloyd launched into a Chicago story about how a crony of his who was a slick poker player, "if there ever was one," had lost $5,000 one night—a lot of money at the time, it during the depression. It was also winter, cold enough to kill anyone who spent more than a few seconds in Lake Michigan, which his crony did after losing, and thus killed himself.

I hadn't heard the story before, but then many of Lloyd's stories came out according to the situation. He was wearing a maroon bow tie that matched his maroon and dark green checked sports jacket and in the pocket was a triangle of a dark green handkerchief. I imagined he had planned to wear it while sitting in the Hotel Utah lobby, that or the one he wore the night we had his friends for dinner—that now seemed so long ago—both in the suitcase tucked away for "the occasion." The fact that he was wearing it in Truckee showed he had spunk in him for what he might have considered a lesser occasion. However, in such a hotel as this, a lesser occasion it was not. I complimented Hank Nelson on the hotel once again, and he was flattered. Mrs. Nelson, who asked us to call her Sally, came out with two large slices of chocolate cake.

"It's snowing quite hard outside," she announced; her blue eyes were full of life, excited about the weather change. She'd have more days of skiing, she said, before summer set in. "Hank doesn't ski, but I love it. I go as often as I can. People here, in town, either go all the way with it like I do, or like Hank, couldn't be bothered."

"I don't like shivering on the lift," Hank said, defending himself, "and I don't like the idea of breaking a leg. It all boils down to not wanting to physically suffer and being realistic. But my wife has been lucky, comes back not shivering and in one piece. The mountain behind us will have the last word on that score and how much snow before passing it on to us here below. One time we had snow in June..." he looked over at his wife.

"Five or six years ago," she said. "The Sierra is unpredictable."

Sally and her husband talked about the strangeness of mountain life, the purity of the air, the vivid colors from being so high, altitudes that are not for everyone, and those who live here are good people, who do not question the life of others, yet ready to help when needed. I recalled Sheriff Montana in that respect. I told her I used to ski when I was growing up in Salt Lake but have not done it for some time.

"One doesn't forget," she said emphatically, looking me straight in the eyes, and I wondered if she was applying this thought to other happenings in her life. We all have our pasts.

Wine, Sally Nelson's dinner, Lloyd and Hank's reflections on the card game of poker, created a long distance from the snow outside, the fact that it would affect our departure, and caused a relaxed and adaptable spirit to any of life's happenings.

"What time do you want to leave tomorrow?" Lloyd asked, maybe having guessed my new adaptability. He, an early riser. Snow, not an issue.

The Nelsons had excused themselves to take care of the other hotel guests who were also invited to dinner.

"You decide," I said.

Suddenly the idea of leaving became a strange, foreign thing. It cut into the well-being like the sun disappearing for a moment from a warmed body. I had to remind myself that we were on our way to Salt Lake. For a while, in this time frame, it seemed I was floating, not directed toward any destination, and this time it was positive. Like a soft white smoke, the Sierra had twisted itself gently around me, and I realized I did not want to leave. But it was Lloyd who was ready to go—he the person who had to be convinced to go on the trip in the first place. Salt Lake being what convinced him.

It had been a long day. My Victorian bed was welcoming in its Victorian surroundings, the curtains had been drawn and the pillows fluffed, a small lamp on the bed stand glowed a soft light, and the bed covers had been folded back showing a wedge of exquisitely white sheets, inviting one to do nothing else in life but to crawl under them.

I had a dream that night. Of course it was about Sheriff Montana. It was a crazy, romantic dream, the dream of a teenager. We were both on a horse, I was seated behind him, arms lightly around his waist, he had his wide-brimmed hat on, and I wanted to lean my head against him, but I didn't. Then he looked around at me and smiled, undid my hands, and pulled me forward, folded my arms across him so I was tight against his back. I rested my head against him. Suddenly we were in a jeep riding through the streets of Truckee, looking for the blue car, and I kept pleading with him to stop because I had seen it on a side street. But he wouldn't. He said it didn't matter.

"It'll follow us," I screamed. But I couldn't make him listen, and he looked over at me and smiled like he did on the horse. I woke up suddenly. My heart was pounding from the effort in trying to make Sheriff Montana believe me about seeing the car on a side street. I lay there trying to pull myself out of the dream, yet not wanting to, thinking back to the part when we were on the horse and he had unlocked my hands and pulled me against him. Finally I drifted off to sleep. In the morning when I woke, the dream had distanced itself, there were still pieces of it that I wanted to keep, but they were slipping away, the pieces polished and waxed, and I could not keep a grip on them.

It was morning, and the loud knocking on the door brought me totally awake.

"Coming."

I quickly slipped into a sweatshirt and pants that had long ago replaced a bathrobe. I opened the door to find Lloyd standing there, newspaper in hand. He was wearing the light blue robe we had picked out together especially for the trip. My morning newspaper left at the door fell in over the threshold.

"Margo, look at this." His face was white as he came in. I swooped my newspaper up from the floor and bent over what he was showing me on the front page of his. In large print, heading a column in the lower half was written: *COUPLE SLAIN IN SANTA CRUZ*. I went on to read it:

An elderly couple was found dead, slain in an apartment of a condominium complex in Santa Cruz, California. Apparently they had been dead for some days, the bodies discovered by the landlord. The couple, Louise and Howard Fuller, had spent time in the apartment sorting out the belongings of the sister of Mr. Fuller, Minnie Clark Watson, who had recently passed away and had resided there. So far there are no suspects. The motive appeared to be robbery due to the disorder found in the apartment. There were no signs of a struggle. Both had been shot in the back. Neighbors were in a state of shock, as the complex is occupied by mostly elderly people and has always been a tranquil living area.

Dazed I found my way across the room and sat on the bed, Lloyd just stood there looking at me.

"Jesus, I can't believe it!" He was still so white, I was afraid he might be ill.

"Here, sit down, Lloyd." I got up and pulled a rigid Victorian chair from a corner for him.

Lloyd sighed heavily, "I wish it were dinner time, so I could have a martini."

I opened my newspaper and spread the front page on the bed, found the article, and read it greedily, as if the piece would have more information than the same one Lloyd had. My hands were icy, and I felt sick.

"Those poor people," Lloyd said. Then, voicing what I was thinking, "It could have been *us*, Margo. They could have robbed *us*...done that to *us*...All of it happened while we were still there, before we left on our trip. They could have decided to come up to us instead."

He looked small and vulnerable in the chair, his blue bathrobe, hastily put on, hung in folds, the one that we decided would fit him at the time, and dangling pitifully from the waist was still the price tag.

I said, my voice a whisper, trying to put some force into it, logic into words for his sake, "First floors are always the ones robbers use. They wouldn't have *come* upstairs. That's one advantage of your living on the second floor."

This reasoning failed to impress Lloyd, nor was I much impressed and had to struggle to keep my voice steady. The thought that we were still there when it happened, along with the real possibility that it could have been us instead of the elderly couple, and tragically enough it was *they* who had been killed, left me feeling weak. Maybe it was true about the stairs. They had saved *us*. But not *them*.

"...they were dead in there, just below us while we were packing. Jesus," he said.

I had flashes of the brother, his wife, talking non-stop to us about his sister, the Santa Cruz Boardwalk that we talked about, their showing us through the house, standing at the door smiling when we left and inviting us to return, their kindness...later sprawled out on the floor somewhere, shot in the back... I forced the picture from my mind as one must do in a state of shock.

"Things like this happen, Lloyd," I said, trying to sound tough, an echo of Lloyd himself, blunt-talking on better days. "Think of the crimes every day that take place. This time it just happened to be close to us."

"...and we had just been talking to them," he went on, not listening to me. "Those poor people...good people."

"I know, I know," unable to find anything else worthwhile to say. There was no way I could turn the situation to make it sound better. How could anything sound better than a gentle couple being shot in the back by a murderer? Lloyd couldn't find anything more to say either, and we both sat dumbly, he in the stiff chair, me on the edge of the bed, both of us staring at the floor. It came then to me, and I dared not voice it: if the murder and the blue car together had meaning or was a coincidence. The thought left me so cold, I wouldn't have been able to pronounce it anyway.

"What a terrible thing," Lloyd said finally. "I want to call Junie."

I, too, thought that was a good idea. Have breakfast, and then after being nourished, I would have to tell Lloyd about the car. The car—or maybe better to wait. For Lloyd it would be a very heavy second shoe that dropped.

I understood his wanting to talk to Junie for I needed someone also, we were in this alone, the two of us, and it would have been good to have had a third party, and Junie, a comfort for Lloyd, would supply also information. When I left Dev, I felt very much alone. I never gave the real reason for leaving to anyone. Who would have understood? No one. They were Vietnamese kids, foreigners, part of the enemy, so the reason we gave were marital differences. Common for a separation. But now Lloyd and I in this room—foreign with Victorian furniture, from the window snow in spring, he with the price tag that our mother would have already eliminated still hanging from his new bathrobe, simulated a different kind of aloneness. I made the decision that I would telephone Sherriff Montana. It was a calming thought. Something to hold onto.

"I'll get dressed and shaved then," Lloyd said standing up.

"Why don't we have breakfast first? It's probably too early to call Junie," I said.

"No! I'll be ready in about a half hour—well, I'll be damned!" he exclaimed suddenly, glancing out the window. "It's still snowing and hard."

We stood at the window collecting ourselves as we watched the flakes thrash, so tightly knit, it seemed we were looking at a solid white sheet against the pane. Vaguely, in the back of my mind, there was a meaning, a coming together, the blue car linked to the murder, but I was too shocked to go into it. *The Sierra*, I thought. What will *she* bring upon us? I had always thought of a great mountain as *she*. But there are many parts to it that make up the Sierra— so written in the hotel brochure left for guests—*she*, used is the whole. *Sierra*, I thought, a name that flows quietly. I thought of the Fullers. How could this have happened? For what reason? Out the window, against the haze of snow, I recalled the nephew, unfriendly, seated on the couch, one capable of...murder? To murder two elderly people could only be the reason: drugs. That is why the place looked like a robbery. Desperation. The murderer was searching for drugs. But the nephew?

Lloyd interrupted, "You know we're not going anywhere today, Margo, and that is the understatement of the year." I didn't answer, he also at the window collecting himself, staring out. Then he continued, "Reminds me of the time in Salt Lake," he began, "you and Nina and your mother were snowed in – before we were married—and I came over to help you shovel. I barely got there when the snow started again. I couldn't leave, even with chains. That was a hard winter, bad in other states, too. We lit a fire, and I spent the night on the couch." He laughed, "Your mother was worried about what the neighbors would say when they spotted my car there the next morning. Let them talk, I told her, but to tell the truth, I worried about it the whole time on the couch. I hardly slept. I was up at five the next norming waiting for the snowplow to come so I could leave. And leave I did. She didn't even hear me."

The incident vaguely came back to me. Most of my memories that winter were not of Lloyd but of the shoveling that Nina and I were assigned to do, a job that seemed endless that year. I did not give much thought, if any, to our mother's romantic attachment, and it never occurred to me that she could have one. I only remembered one time, and it came to me now as it did occasionally in my life: our mother sitting on my bed, her face silvery in the dark. Awake I must have heard her when she came in, for she had been out on her first date and it was with Lloyd. She had stopped to say goodnight. It was only later, as a more perceptive adult, that I suspected it was she who had awakened me, purposely, for she was bursting to talk about the evening and I was the older daughter, the girlfriend she needed for those moments. Young-looking and beautiful, she told me about the party she had been to and the man she had met. I had barely listened to her about the evening, for I was only taken by her happiness, her beauty, the glow in her face. Her face silver and pure in the darkness of the room. Never had I seen her so lovely. This I recalled as Lloyd, and I stood at the window, the flakes falling. But I would never tell him. A story too poignant. It might have made him sad.

"Shucks, it seems like everything happens at once now with this snow," he said, still at the window.

"We don't have anyone waiting for us, Lloyd. We are free to make decisions." This I felt only too well.

"Yes, that is the case," he pronounced matter-of-factly.

I said, "We'll just have to make the best of it. I have some books I bought in Santa Cruz so I can read. You know what you can do."

"What?"

"Play poker with the Nelsons."

"I'll have to force myself to be good company after what happened to the poor Fullers."

"Maybe a good card game or two will help," I said.

After Lloyd left, it occurred to me that I should check the car. Make sure the doors were locked. I took out his other set of keys from my purse—what Lloyd did on our visits so Nina and I could use his car for our purposes, he not bothered looking for his own keys to lend us. I was beginning, with relief, to give no importance to the blue car being related to the murder. To begin with, Lloyd and I were not the only ones to have talked with the couple before we left, which excluded us of being sole witnesses—if the car was following us for that reason. I recalled our dinner conversation with Lloyd's friends, and Wavey had mentioned she had talked to Mr. Fuller. As probably others had talked to them, too. That reason for the car following us, I concluded, not related to the murder. This last reasoning left me brave enough to check all the windows, if tightly shut, as we had not imagined snow. I also withdrew my thought to call Sheriff Montana. I had no proof of anything and kind as he was I felt he was making an effort to believe me—someone off the street who came to him saying she was being followed. Who could blame him?

I hurriedly got dressed, put on the only shoes I had for the snow, which were my sneakers. Good sneakers, however, and could take a bit of snow.

5.

IN SPITE OF LACKING THE PROPER CLOTHES, I FOUND THE COLD AIR outside inviting, the whole of the storm enjoyable, even if it caused our departure to be postponed. The snowstorms that inevitably brought bothers to us residents in Salt Lake did not affect my life there. In my heart, I never minded them. I liked the feeling of isolation that a storm gives, the touch of class in the quietness as it went about creating something that resulted in layers and layers of still, white beauty. There was no white as pure as freshly fallen snow, no particles as light as a few of those flakes on the finger-tip, and if you blew on them, they would flicker away more feathery than airy dandelions. It had been a while that we had had a good one in Washington, the winters drizzly and cold, or just plain cold and below zero.

As I did not have boots, I chose my steps carefully. The Nelsons had cleared the sidewalk all the way from the front to around the parking in back, though the results of their work was again covered by a light layer of white. My feet crunched on it, the sound sharp in the stillness. There were few cars passing on this secondary street in front of the hotel, but a plow had already been through, cleared and dropped sand. You knew a snow country when you saw one. If this were Washington, it would have taken a whole day, maybe two, for the plow to get to the secondary roads, supermarkets would be half empty, and the schools, of course, including mine, would be closed. The flakes were falling so fast that air and sky had become one, the flakes dry, and they layered quickly, telling me this was not to be a mushy winter storm that would melt in a day. I reminded myself this was the Sierra, and storms here were not usually wimps.

I checked the windows of the car, that were closed, then decided to turn on the engine, roll the car back and forth a few times to flatten the snow around it, thereby make our exit easier. Probably a useless thing to do, but it still felt good to be outdoors, coupled with the wise idea to do what I could in preventing the car from becoming stuck. Determined to avoid a complicated departure, I would come out later and do it again.

The car balked at going back. I got out to check the tires and found the left rear one flat. Checking it further, I saw the tire was slashed. A long slash to make sure the job was done right. I stared at it a moment, trying to absorb the fact. I had never been the victim of an act of aggression, and now that it had happened, it left me with an odd, queer feeling. The act was personal and violating. Who would do it? But as I knelt beside the tire, the snowflakes falling benignly around me, settling gently on my shoulders, the backs of my sneakers, I knew it had to do with the blue car.

I struggled to calm the fear that kept me rooted beside the tire—fright does wondrous things sometimes, it can cause one to instinctively react and run, or it can paralyze, for by being paralyzed one acquires a false aura of protection, nothing will happen as long as one doesn't move. Rabbits do this. How long I knelt there seemed time stood still. Longer than some seconds and long enough for me to become cold and the car key as ice in my hand; long enough for me to feel the sense of being alone, that whoever did this was not far, and now seriously frightened, I rose, ran through the lot, slipping and sliding along the shoveled sidewalk that brought me to the front of the hotel.

Once inside I went into the last degree of calming myself for there was Lloyd at the door waiting for me in his plaid jacket and another bow tie.

"What's going on? What're you doing outside, Margo? You don't even have boots on!"

I looked down at my sneakers that were covered with snow. The icy cold was seeping through my stockings.

"I had to check the car. Make sure the windows were closed."

"Sure they were. I had already checked them."

"When?"

"After dinner before I went to bed."

I should have guessed it. Not bothered by the cold, he probably went out in his shirtsleeves, too.

Under normal circumstances, I would have been angry with him, reprimanded him because he could have slipped, broken a leg, and then aside from that happening brought on by himself, where would we have been? Certainly not on our way to Utah.

At the moment, only one thing I had to say, "Did you see anyone, Lloyd?"

"See anyone? Who would I see?"

"If you ran into anyone else rolling up car windows in the cold," I joked, trying to make light of my question.

"Now that you mention it, there was a car leaving as I came in the lot."

"What kind?" I asked warily. "One of the many jeeps in town?"

"Oh, I don't know. I think it was a blue car. Yes, now that you asked, it was because it looked like the same one behind us when we left Santa Cruz. It was behind us for a while and I…" he went on slowly, "then…I…well…forgot about it."

He stopped and looked at me. We both stared at each other.

Hank Nelson came up to us, directing his question to Lloyd, "Say, did you get you driver's license worked out with the sheriff yesterday?"

"Driver's license?"

"Your daughter was telling me you left it at home. She went to see our sheriff about it."

"Why, I have it here with me," Lloyd said, looking with wonder at Hank Nelson, then at me.

"He found it," I laughed, quickly changing the subject to the snow, the plows, and Washington problems with snow. Hank Nelson fell into it. Lloyd was quiet.

"How about some coffee and your table's set for breakfast. You look darn cold," Hank said, eyes resting on my feet. "What'd you do, go outside like that?"

"I checked the windows of the car," I said, an easy answer finally one being true. "I'm going upstairs to change my shoes," I said. "I'll be down in a minute."

Lloyd made a move to come with me. "Margo…"

"I'll meet you at the table, Lloyd."

In my room, I took my shoes off, dropped my socks on the floor, and where had I put the telephone number of Sheriff Montana? For a moment, I felt a touch of panic and told myself to calm down. I felt in the pocket of my jeans I had on and found it in the back pocket. His home number because he said he was not going to be in his office today. It was not late. I prayed he was still home.

I held the piece of paper under the table-lamp next to the bed. One of the digits could be a nine or a four. I couldn't tell. There was no phonebook in the room. Should I try both or just plain ask the desk for his home number? Time was passing. Lloyd was downstairs waiting, wondering what was going on about the car, the lie about his license, and soon to be informed about the slashed tire. I picked up the phone, gave a try on the readable digit.

The phone rang. No answer.

And if he wasn't there? What would be the next step? I pictured the act of aggression, imagined the person heading for the car, carrying something that would cut through a thick tire…

Guessing the unclear digit, I dialed. It rang four times while I feared he was sleeping or the digit wrong. He picked up.

"I'm sorry to bother you. This is Margo Heston…if you remember from yesterday and a car?"

"Sure, I remember. Things going okay?"

I told him about the slashed tire and the murder that took place in Santa Cruz and then the morning caved in on me. I made an attempt to finish and couldn't.

"Hey, I understand. Now take a deep breath."

I did and tried to laugh. "I just didn't know who to turn to…I thought…" but my voice would not stay steady.

"This is what a sheriff is for. I'll be there in ten minutes. I want to tell Hank and Sally about this before coming. I'll give them a call. They should know why a sheriff is coming to talk to you early in the morning. Would seem strange just about a driver's license. Where will you and your step-father be?"

"In the dining-room. He's waiting for me to come down for breakfast in the dining room."

"Good. I'll join you for coffee. Knowing Sally she's already fixing you breakfast. You must eat something. You've had a scare."

I draped my wet socks over the radiator and found others, changed from wet jeans to another pair and brought out dry shoes, packed at the last minute from home—I thanked luck for that reminder, and it probably was our mother. Along with easy clothes for Santa Cruz life, I had shopped in Santa Cruz for upgrades—thoughts of the Hotel Utah. Black leather upgrades, tie shoes, not for snow, but they would do.

In the dining room, Lloyd was drinking his coffee and smoking a cigarette. I sat down across from him.

"I asked Hank to bring you a cup of coffee." He looked displeased.

"Thanks, Lloyd. The sheriff is coming. Sheriff Montana."

"About my license that I never lost? I don't get any of this. What's going on? It's about that damn car, isn't it?"

"I didn't want to tell you, Lloyd. I didn't want to worry you. Yes, it's about the car. It followed us here. And now that I know you saw it means the car was following us from Santa Cruz since you were driving then. On my turn driving, I tried different times to shake it on the highway but couldn't. I thought maybe when we turned off for Truckee it would have finally gone on, but it didn't. I saw it at the top of the hotel street after you went in to register. It was then I decided to go to the police—Sheriff. Because Truckee is a small town, he's called Sheriff. And since it's rather strange that as soon as a hotel guest arrives and asks where the sheriff's office is, I made up the excuse of your license being lost."

"And you did go to see the sheriff?"

"When I said I was going out for a walk, I really did go to see the sheriff."

"And all this time you didn't tell me." He shook his head and stamped out his cigarette. "Why didn't you tell me when we were in the car and you thought we were being followed?"

"It wouldn't have changed anything while we were driving. And Lloyd, you're eighty-three-years-old. Worries like that you don't need. Especially at the wheel of a car on a road trip."

"Oh, come on, Margo, I'm not going to drop dead just because I'm a little worried. I could have eased your mind by convincing you the car probably was having some kind of a problem."

"Lloyd, that could not have been the case. The car was waiting for us at the exit of the place where we had stopped to eat lunch. It did not lack mobility as a sign of car problems."

"The car was waiting at the exit? All that time, sitting there waiting for us to finish lunch...? Then it went on to follow us? Well, that's a different story."

There was no point in hiding anything more from him in view of the fact that Sheriff Montana was coming—and in view of the fact with Sheriff Montana I was going to have to bring up something even more serious—the slashed tire.

"This morning when I went out to check the car," I continued, "I found the rear left tire slashed."

I watched my coffee as I stirred it, not to see what this information was doing to him.

"You said the sheriff's coming NOW?" he asked. "For a slashed tire?" I looked up at him. He was grim but in no danger of physically suffering from the tire information. This heartened me.

"Yes, I called him when I was upstairs changing my shoes."

"What's your impression of him? Not that I'm convinced we need one."

"I don't have much of one yet. He's patient. We drove around town looking for the car, so he could check the license, but we didn't see it. He was kind enough to do that because I don't think he was very convinced. I can't quite blame him. He gave me his phone number at home in case something came up. There wasn't much else he could do. By the way, he was the source for your Cokes when I told him I was going to pick a few up on the way back to the hotel. They were from last summer, and he apologized because they weren't cold. I told him not to worry because you liked them lukewarm. So that's also the story of your Cokes."

"Very thoughtful of him. But getting back to his coming here, I don't know what he can do. What can he do about a slashed tire? Now with this snow...I'd like to have a re-deal on our whole trip. We should have stayed home, Margo."

I didn't know what to say to that. Would we be alive if we had done so? With a choice, I would have picked a car following us than the risk of not having left Lloyd's apartment because we were dead. Lloyd's flight of stairs wouldn't stop one determined. Could be the stairs would have saved us. No one likes stairs when in a hurry.

Sheriff Montana suddenly appeared at our table. I looked up and smiled, flustered and embarrassed after my losing it with him on the telephone. And I was still frightened with hands still shaking that I kept between my knees under the table.

I introduced him to Lloyd, who on his very best behavior stood up to shake his hand, and asked him to sit down. At that moment, Hank Nelson came over with coffee. He sat down with us. There was nothing to do but be patient, put on hold telling Sheriff Montana what I remembered about the couple, and our visit at the Fullers.

Hank Nelson and his wife were hospitable, and I could see how they had turned to the hotel business. It was second nature to them, even if Californians had a way of making one feel welcome they went one step further. Conversation was about the snow and our not being able to get off as we had planned. Suddenly one more day in town became tolerable for Lloyd when Hank talked about building up the fire in the dining room and playing poker.

"Sally is around someplace and she's not going skiing until tomorrow, and maybe we can get our other guests to play. What about you, Mike? Up for a game of poker today?"

"Depends on how the day goes. Anyway," he said, looking at Lloyd, then me, "Hank wins all the time. But Sally compensates as a cook."

Hank Nelson stood up. Affectionately he laid his hand on Sheriff Montana's shoulder, "This man can do a lot of things, but he's not one who shines in the kitchen department."

There was a bond between the two men, the type of friendly bond that I can imagine one finds in a small town where pasts have been closely shared, good and bad. Since Sheriff Montana had told them about the Santa Cruz murder and the slashed tire, Hank Nelson did not let on. I appreciated the discreetness when he rose from the table and told Lloyd he hoped to see him later. To talk about it around the table was to keep my voice under control and probably couldn't.

Sally Nelson arrived with breakfast. I had forgotten about eating until I saw it, the beauty of bacon, sausages, a large plate of scrambled eggs, warm toast in a basket covered with a soft-red cloth, all keeping company with a bowl of fresh cut fruit.

Sally Nelson said, "I wasn't sure what you liked, so decided to make bacon and eggs. I figured one can't go wrong with tradition."

Oh, how good it was. The snow falling, the fire that Hank Nelson lit, a corner in life that would close when we went on to reality, but now we ate with full hunger, and I will never remember what we talked about, perhaps Truckee. Lloyd might have had one of his stories, but an extraordinary sense of well-being prevailed. I knew my mother had a hand in it, as she did years ago when I couldn't find Lloyd's car at the beach parking lot and then was drawn to it. There's a spirit-world out there, it got me back to the hotel entrance from the slashed tire without falling, rather than me frozen on the ground and later discovered. I was allowed to leave that scene in one piece. We also slipped easily into first names without formally suggesting it. I've always observed that Lloyd's name was easy, fit him without his last, and I've rarely heard anyone call him Mr. Edwards. Even after introduced.

On a last round of coffee, Mike suggested we go to one of our rooms and talk as it was too public here. Lloyd suggested his room, and I was grateful as I had a quick vision of socks and jeans drying wherever, as well as wet sneakers and generally a room not picked up for visitors.

In his room, Lloyd pulled out one of the Victorian chairs for Mike, pulled out the second Victorian chair for me while he used the desk-chair. The three of us sat.

"Okay then. Let's start back from Santa Cruz. I was going to read about it in my office," he said to me, "when you called. Santa Cruz is a small town, so it must have been a shock to you both. Robberies, these kinds of crimes, are hard to solve. Someone comes off the street out of nowhere, performs thievery, and in this case worse, then disappears the same way. No one sees the person leave, and in ten minutes, that's it, all blended in with the world."

Quietly I said, "They were killed in the apartment under Lloyd's."

Mike looked stunned. For one whole moment, I took pleasure in the turn of events, threatening and tragic as they were, that proved I was not flaky. I went on to explain that we had gone down to see the apartment because Lloyd might have been interested in moving there and was also interested in the rug. I told him about the Fullers, their friendliness, how they had been searching for his sister's will, then felt sure it was her money she had hidden. That she never had a will. Then guardedly I brought up the nephew. I knew what I was going to say could have meaning and not good. But perhaps important. Yet if innocent…

"There was someone else in that apartment while we were there."

I felt both of them watching me carefully.

"Lloyd," I went on grimly, responding to the astonishment that had crept into his face, we forgot all about him. The *nephew* This morning while I was reading about it in the newspaper, something bothered me. Later I remembered the nephew.

Lloyd said, "I forgot all about him." He was still sitting in the desk chair, rose, then sat down again, "Damn. He'd been so quiet, he hadn't made any impression on me. They introduced him—who did they say he was, Margo?"

"As I recall, Mr. Fuller said he was the son of his dead brother. Didn't say the nephew's name. Only introduced him as a nephew. I had the feeling they didn't want to, were embarrassed about him. I could imagine their being uncomfortable, he looked sullen, and to be honest, not very clean. His only interest was in the can of beer he was drinking. What bothered me was the strange look to his eyes and the way they followed us as we were leaving. It certainly wasn't out of disappointment since he hadn't shown any interest in us until then. His unfriendliness was a contrast to Mr. and Mrs. Fuller, who were talkative and pleasant. We were rude, I'm afraid. Because they talked so much, we left too abruptly. Now I'm sorry about it."

Mike smiled, "There's a saying, 'Hindsight is life's barb.' Do you think anyone else knew he was there?"

"As far as I know, I don't think so," I said. "Before leaving we had some of Lloyd's friends for dinner—three of them live in the same condo compound. The subject of the couple came up. I told them about our looking at the apartment, talking to the husband and wife who were there. I recall Wavey, one of Lloyd's friends that evening at dinner, had talked with them, too. I briefly brought up the nephew, but no one had seen him around. I don't think the Fullers had mentioned him to Wavey, and we, ourselves, had only seen him on that one visit—oh, I'm wrong. Just before our trip I was coming back from town and saw him outside in front of the deceased sister's apartment. He had a suitcase, and to my surprise, looked clean and shaved. We each raised a hand in greeting and just then a taxi pulled up, he got in and left. Probably not important, but I noticed the door behind him to the apartment was shut, and I thought it was odd that Mr. Fuller was not in the doorway to bid him goodbye or was waiting with him until the cab came. Maybe they had said their good-byes inside." I looked at Lloyd, "Did I leave anything out?"

"Not as far as I'm concerned. Maybe just all the talk that evening at dinner about money and wills. Seems that was of interest to everyone except me. At my age, I like to think of other things. One of our guests who knew Minnie, the sister who passed away, said she had a lot of money. As Margo said, they didn't think she left a will. And I recall her brother said she didn't like lawyers. Fuller said she liked to do treasure hunts. He thought maybe it was one of her games to hide all her money. She had a big painting of a treasure chest on a wall, so could be he wasn't far off base with that idea. I'll add something about the decorations in the apartment and that is they seemed childish to me. It was like she hadn't grown up. But then who am I to be an expert on womens' taste?" Lloyd concluded. "And I can't say much about the guy on the couch, the nephew, except he didn't look too clean. Only that's Santa Cruz for you."

"Now, what about the car? Does Lloyd know about the one following you?"

"I'll answer that one for you, and yes, she did tell me and should have told me earlier," Lloyd said irritably.

"I know how you feel, but it probably wouldn't have done any good then while driving. Two worries sometimes don't make a plus," Mike said. "Tell me what *you* know about the car. If you had noticed it at any time after you left Santa Cruz."

"I'll tell you what I *don't* know and that is if it was there just when we left the town of Santa Cruz. But I saw it *after* we were on the highway and I was driving. "

Mike said, "Do you recall if it was soon after you were on the highway? I know it's difficult to remember, probably because it wasn't important at the time."

"I can give it a shot and say maybe it was not long after we were on the highway. But I didn't think anything of it until now and Margo mentioned it. And then when she told me it was there waiting at the exit after lunch, that was another thing."

Mike said, "I think that we should give a call to the police in Santa Cruz." Feeling the air grown tense, he quickly added, "Now don't be concerned either of you. I'm sure there's nothing to any of it, but I do think that what Margo's just said about this nephew, seeing him outside the apartment, deserves some attention. Suddenly for the police, you both have become witnesses. Could be he's perfectly innocent and by now they've found the person. Your worries would be over. At least *that* one. What I want you to do is start at the beginning; let's go over the whole thing once more. I want to be completely sure I have your account straight. I want you to hang tight because you may be questioned over the telephone."

I looked over at Lloyd. He seemed to be doing better than I. He was watching Sheriff Montana with keen interest.

"Look, it's okay," Mike said to me. Reassuringly he rested his hand a moment on my arm.

We went through our whole visit again with the Fullers. Our going downstairs to take a look at the apartment, seeing the nephew on the couch, Mike interrupting us, asking us to describe the nephew once more, Minnie's "childish taste" as Lloyd said, Lloyd and I trying to combine our observations in that sense.

"No, there was nothing I remember about his face," I concluded once more.

"He needed a shave," Lloyd said.

"What else, Lloyd?" Mike asked.

"He looked thin. I thought that he looked like some of those hippies around at the time in Santa Cruz. Some of them looked half-starved. Though they had one up on the nephew because all of them had beards."

Mike looked amused, turned thoughtful. "Unfortunately drugs can never be discounted, it has its dark corners. But not to jump to conclusions either. I wonder if he lived around there. But if you saw him leaving in a cab with a suitcase… So to conclude, when you met them in the sister's apartment, Mr. Fuller and his wife had the impression his sister, Minnie, had not left a will but her money in cash. In other words, for them a possibility. And they were looking for the will or cash. When you met them in Minnie's apartment."

Lloyd and I both agreed.

"Then the brother talked about his father, his being the engineer in the construction of the roller coaster on the boardwalk in Santa Cruz? That's all you can remember?"

I said, "That's all. But because I showed interest in the roller coaster, Mr. Fuller's wife kindly gave me a sheet of information she had found on the boardwalk—its history about the roller coaster. She had come upon it in Minnie's kitchen drawer. Altogether we must have been there about an hour."

"You didn't see any other rooms?"

"They showed us the whole apartment. The floor plan is the same as mine," Lloyd said.

"Any more comments on that?" Mike asked.

"She had a fixation on decorating, that's all I can say," said Lloyd. "But to each his/her own."

"Would you recognize the nephew if you saw him again?'

Lloyd and I looked at each other; almost simultaneously we said no.

"Okay. I'll give Santa Cruz a call. I'll be back in a few minutes."

I watched him leave, pass through the wintry, diffused light that came from the wide window in Lloyd's room. Beyond the window were tall pines now heavy with snow. The snow had tapered off to a few flakes spinning in the air, and I could catch a glimpse of stately mountain peaks looming not too far in the distance. Truckee, I thought, small town in the middle of nowhere—if one discounts the Sierra, Mike Montana, in his sheepskin jacket and wide-brimmed hat, the patience he was using with Lloyd and myself—and behind the hotel, in the parking lot, Lloyd's car with a slashed tire giving a reason to be afraid, and I was. Murder, car, snowstorm, all of it following us like a string of tin cans tied to a fender.

"It's been twenty years since I've seen a good snowstorm, "Lloyd said. "I've missed it. You remember the deer who used to come in our backyard? Too hungry to be afraid? We were so close to the mountains behind us that we were their first stop. Sometimes I'd just stand there and watch them, wishing there was something I could do to help. One time there was a small one with its mother. It was pitiful, so thin and weak following her around. Nina couldn't stand to watch it. That was when your mother and I had some hay brought in—others were doing it in Salt Lake. You remember those bundles of hay in the backyard?"

"I remember all that hay," I said, touched by the story, Lloyd's confession of soft-heartedness. "I don't remember the part about the fawn though. Did it come back?"

"Never saw it again. That was a damn winter if there ever was one. In a lot of places, they had to drop food from planes to the animals in Nevada and

Arizona. In spite of that, a lot of animals died from starvation. But the cold? It never bothered me. Salt Lake couldn't hold a candle to Chicago."

Giving into the temptation to bring up Boston where one could count on snow each winter and the retirement home Nina found for him, I said laughing, "You could always move to Boston."

"I let myself in for that one, didn't I? Junie and I…would she want to move away from her sister? She wouldn't do that. You and Nina have been quiet about it, but I know what you think. I'm fine where I am. At least before this murder thing. Now what if they never catch whoever did it? Hell, anybody could come in and rob us. What could I do but just sit there? And not only rob, he killed them, too."

"They'll find the person, Lloyd." This I stated emphatically, forcing belief in me.

"Maybe he was the driver of that car. You know what I think, Margo, I think he was. We were the only ones who saw him. Now he's following us. If that wasn't enough, then he slashed the tire. What else does he have in mind?"

Lloyd was only underlining what I felt in my heart to be the case, what I did not want to think about. That soon we would be on our way to Salt Lake once more, and then what?

Mike came back. He looked sober, but when he saw us, he smiled. He kept the smile all the way over to his Victorian chair. I was grateful to him but did not feel reassured.

"The Santa Cruz chief of police is on the phone and wants to talk to you," he looked from me to Lloyd. "Which one of you wants to talk to him?"

Lloyd started to rise, then said, "You go, Margo. You are the one who saw the nephew last. When he left."

I stood up. Mike laid his hand lightly on my shoulder, "They don't have anything on their record about another person in the apartment besides the couple. Just tell him what you told me. Most of all, if you can recall the day, date, you saw him leave in a taxi. Either they were dead when he left or alive."

With horror I remembered the nephew raising his hand in greeting me when I passed, only now there was the possibility that the Fullers were then dead in the apartment.

"Mike," I said, "they must have been alive. He couldn't have killed them then left in plain sight."

Quietly he said, "One thing at a time. You never know about people. We'll go over it again later," for he surely recognized the horror I felt. "I know right now," he continued, "it's difficult to recall on the telephone important information when asked. Do the best you can. How long they had been dead hasn't yet been established. Why don't you take the call to your room without the two of us sitting here. You could think more clearly."

When I came back, Lloyd looked up from talking to Mike. He said, "We forgot to tell Mike about Minnie's two husbands, even though now they're dead and gone. What did Carol May say, the second one married her for her money? In that case, she must have been pretty well off. A single woman with a lot of money. That makes a victim if there ever was one."

"How'd it go?" Mike asked

"I told him what I told you. Only I wasn't quite sure about the date I saw the nephew outside. Now I remember, after hanging up, it was the day after we had friends of Lloyd's for dinner. I had come back from town and found the nephew in front of Minnie's condo. I remember that the shades were pulled and something else—no one was in front to wave him off as he was leaving. It seemed unusual. Especially since he was a relative."

"Do you remember the date?" Mike asked. "The date, the day after your dinner?"

"It was April 6th," Lloyd broke in.

"That was quick," Mike laughed.

"That due to the fact," said Lloyd, "the day after our dinner, on April 6th, I made our reservations to stop here. Thank the Lord. Who knows where we would have ended up with this car following us and the snow?"

"That date," said Mike, "will make the nephew a suspect or prove he isn't. And yes, if you hadn't stopped here, you would have been in a pretty big snowfall. Without chains. What information we have has been given to Santa Cruz. Tomorrow they want to send a detective here to Truckee to talk in person to you both regarding any more information. I said to wait a day." He stopped and looked at each of us for a moment, "I feel that the car following you, the tire, and the murder are linked. As sheriff I'm here for you, and we'll get to the bottom of it. You as possible witnesses will be under police protection, and the hotel bill will be covered. Also, I'll have the car towed and the tire fixed. Checked for fingerprints, if possible. The one who slashed the tire doesn't want you to leave. Obviously wants something from you otherwise..."

"Otherwise," Lloyd finished for him, "he would've taken care of us right away."

"That's a good supposition, Lloyd. Another one is if you left, he'd follow—more truth to that than a supposition. Here you're both safe while we wait to see what the next move will be. Because this person *will* make one. Soon. I feel it in my bones." He smiled, "Indian instinct. What you must do is not to leave the hotel without me. Lloyd won't mind that. I'm sure he has no intention of taking a stroll in the snow."

"Don't be so sure," I said dismally. "He likes snow. Lloyd, it just came to me there is something important that we forgot. The purple envelope!"

"The purple envelope? Damn, that's right! They came across it while we were there. On the front was written *HUNT.*"

"Tell me about it," said Mike.

We explained what Mr. Fuller had said about the envelope, his sister using colored ones so they could be seen on a treasure hunt. We agreed it was an original way of hiding money—a single woman who had a lot, with an imagination, and an easy way for the Fullers, when they found it, to avoid wills.

Mike said, "It could be important or not much. Whoever killed them probably found that the couple had come across the money, killed them for it, then left. So envelopes wouldn't matter. Let me add that the sun will come out soon, and in a day or so, all this information will be recorded and you will be able to continue on to Salt Lake. I personally will be behind you for a few miles to make sure you aren't followed. Trust me."

I knew he was right about our staying on in Truckee. I believed what he said and that he would keep us safe, this seemed as sure to me as the pines through the window now thickly covered with snow, the milk-white light in the room with touches of chrome yellow not yet bright enough to convince the snowfall to fade away. His eyes, black in the growing light of the room, were of his own people, the space between that time and the present had become shortened, the distance now fluid and mattered less. What remained through centuries was the given word and still strong.

My attraction to Dev had not been like this. With Dev it had been comfortable, and he was, after all, a handsome veteran returning from Vietnam. A hero, as those who returned all were from fighting their hearts out in a land unknown, different from Europe in that sense, jungles and more jungles, fever and insects, enemies without uniforms so could not be distinguished, those enemies who knew well their land, in life used to hardships, and in war, that a strong defense. In marriage we moved quietly and steadily forward, facing problems—that were not extraordinary but what a normal half-a-lifetime brings—solving them. A goal was children. Yet I had never experienced a flame burning. Never with Dev. Ours was a safe, reliable relationship. Marriage had been as a still pond. No ruffles, little life to it; we rarely even fought, we discussed. We had been biding our time, or perhaps I had. For what unknown? Had I right now not been sitting in a room with Mike Montana, I would never had had these present thoughts.

I said, "I'm not one for venturing out on the highway again. I'm sure you aren't either, Lloyd."

"Well, we don't have a car for one thing. I don't discount that a tire would have to be ordered and would take a while. And by the way, there's a ballgame on right now in New York—we're three hours behind in California."

"Hank will turn it on in the living room," Mike said. "If not on already. He's a baseball person, too."

Lloyd got up from his chair. "I'll go find him."

Mike looked at me, sized me up, "You'll need something for the snow. If you want, we can go out and get something to tide you over. Boots, something warmer to wear. Maybe you could use them in Salt Lake. On the way, I'll show you around the great metropolis of Truckee in daylight. There's nothing we can do right now except to keep you both safe. Lloyd is fine here, you're with a sheriff, and we'll let the day play out and check later Santa Cruz."

The words *Salt Lake* brought life into focus again. It had slipped into my subconscious. For the last twenty-four hours, my world had stopped here, beyond had eclipsed. There had been only Truckee and danger.

I followed Mike into the living room to tell Lloyd. He was there with Hank, both watching the ball game. There was loud cheering, so there must have been something important. Maybe a home run. It brought back the times I had gone to games with my grandfather to see The Salt Lake City Bees play. Many on the team were Mexicans, not tall but fast. It seemed they could run from one plate to another in seconds; I ate peanuts from the shell with a Coke and had a crush on one of the Mexican pitchers. The Bees had a good reputation, and there was always someone who hit a homer at the game—one time it was my hero, the pitcher.

"Lloyd," I whispered to him, "Mike is going to take me to look for boots. We'll be back soon. Was it a homer?"

"Yes and the wrong team. Get yourself some warm clothes, Margo. It's not Santa Cruz."

Mike said the same thing to Hank and we'd be back soon.

"You're taking her to Laura's?"

"I'm thinking of that. After the boots."

While I went to my room to get my jacket, Mike went outside to check the tire.

"Yes," he said when I met him downstairs, "it has a big gash in it. He must have had something useful in his car to do it. Probably took him a bit of time also. You don't go through a tire easily if you want to make a sizeable slit. It'll have to be taken to the garage, but Lloyd is here for taking care of it. Maybe he's wrong and they'll have a replacement without ordering a new tire. Is that okay with you?"

"Of course," I said. "I'm sure for Lloyd the sooner, the better to move on. And we're both grateful, Mike."

6.

OUTSIDE IT HAD STOPPED SNOWING, BUT EVERYWHERE IT WAS ankle-deep. The flakes now spun slowly in the air without purpose anymore, and likewise I forced my feelings toward Mike grow neutral. We had our own lives, he with another woman, who I imagined we would presently see, and mine—well, I had not quite figured mine out but with time…

"You're going to soak your feet," Mike said at the front door. "I'll wait at the bottom of the steps," which were clear, and he descended ahead of me and waited. When I got to the last step, he swooped me up.

"I'll carry you to the jeep. No reason to trudge through the snow. We'll park right in front of the shoe store. In Truckee one doesn't have to worry much about parking spaces in the morning." Still holding me, he opened the car door and carefully set me on the seat.

"I've only seen this done in movies," I laughed.

"How do you think I learned?"

"The name Sheriff fits here in the mountains," I said when he got in the car. "It's easy to imagine how it was in the days of the *Gold Rush*—I was informed about it in the hotel brochure," I admitted. "If someone came back from that era, he or she might find not so much changed." I looked over at him, "There's still a sheriff. Who is taking me to buy boots in a town I've never been in before—not to dwell on the reason."

"You're right. Not much has changed," he said, starting the car. "Tourists who come here are usually on their way somewhere else, so there's not much incentive to expand. As far as I'm concerned, that's fine. Expansion means more jobs, and that's good, but more people and pollution. A selfish way to look at it, I guess. Over there," he said as we passed slowly along the main street, "is the Veteran's Memorial Building."

I followed his indication. It was not a very interesting one: a bland yellow, steel-roofed, neutral type of building.

He pulled up in front of it. "An example of the ignorance of man, how his choice of replacement can result in an eyesore. The Memorial Building was built on the site of the Mcglashen Mansion. Now why the mansion had to be torn down, I don't know. Mcglashen was at one time editor of *The Truckee Republican*. He also wrote an excellent book on the history of the Donner Party. You've probably heard something about their tragedy."

I said I heard about the Donner Party. No details except that they had broken a trail—to be later used by the Mormons—through a mountain in Utah, now referred to as Emigration Canyon. A mountain that loomed behind our house in Salt Lake, I added. We laughed over that fact of irony.

"When kids," I said, "we all knew Emigration Canyon had to do with the Donner Party, but on the other hand, it was also the place that had a dam, and we could ice skate on it. I hadn't dwelled on the story—after all we were just kids—but one time there were only a few of us skating, and I had a strong feeling of being surrounded. It seemed very real to me. I stopped and looked up, saw the trees looming with their heavy shadows on the snow and knew there were people in wagons, women walking in long skirts climbing over rocks, children, all following a trail that had to be newly-made as they continued forward, everything cold and frightening. And I was among *them*. The experience of feeling it all, being part of it, lasted a minute. It was haunting. I never went back there to ice skate. It is beyond the imagination how the Donner Party made a trail through the mountain. A lasting trail because the Mormons later followed it. How they all did it and made it out through the canyon? Endurance and determination. And after all that, they died in the Sierras."

"When you think about it," he said, "there are centuries of pasts always there in mountains. As living things a need to share for a minute when you were ice skating. It's nice to look at it that way. What memories they all have.

George Donner," Mike said, "had made bad decisions, plus they had had a rotten deal with the weather. An early snowfall. If they had arrived in the Sierras only a couple of days earlier, they would have missed the storm. Made it out to Sacramento. But after the canyon, it was the Salt Flats that slowed them down. Hard to imagine wagons going over that soft ground, which was what did them in. Snow began just after they arrived in the Sierras, finally got so deep, they couldn't hunt and what they had they soon finished. When the rescue team arrived, they found only half the party. The rest had perished. Including George Donner."

Mike continued, "Now there' a highway in place of the trail with a sign written *Donner's Summit*, just a name for an interested tourist, and there is no way to imagine how it was. One would have to stand in snow that is feet deep, and it's still snowing, so you can't hunt, there's no way to stay warm because a fire melts the snow and makes puddles around it and always the hunger. And," he said softly, "that was how it was."

I hadn't even noticed that we had been sitting parked for a while. I had visualized all he had said, easily helped by the feet of snow around us that had fallen in the past hours. For a few minutes, we sat without saying anything, and the silence enfolded us naturally. It was fitting.

He broke the stillness.

"Snow's left a strong past in this part of the country. It can be an enemy like the sea is, and you can't work against it. You can only work with it. But even then…They learned how to carve into it for the railroad, and it would let them, then they'd hit a drift and those old-fashioned rotary plows would break, it would snow again and it would take swarms of manpower to get through the stuff once more. All of that was what Nature wanted. She wanted to show us she couldn't be overpowered so easily: we are the subjects—she reigns. We shouldn't forget it, but we do. Nature and the Sierra: creation, power, death, and beauty. We humans come and go, the Sierra lives on." He stopped and laughed, "Here we are sitting in front of the store while I'm talking about history and getting philosophical."

"I like to hear about courage," I said. "I've never really been tested. I've never been through life-threatening situations. I don't think we know who we are until we've been tested. And you? What about you? Have you been tested living up here in Sierra country?"

"A time was skiing. I'm sorry to say it was my fault. I went off course. You don't do that when you know you shouldn't. Like the bad judgement of George Donner who had choices. I could hear the avalanche, it makes a slow rumble, and on a clear, sunny day, you know it's not a storm brewing.

"There's no time I can tell you. I must have skied just a few yards before it got me. Interesting how instinct takes over when your life is hanging; you either look for a weapon, or when an avalanche hits, you start to grope. A natural defense. In doing that, I was making breathing space. In an avalanche, it's like a person drowning, your arms naturally fling out because you *are* drowning. When the snow settled, I had room around my face to breathe, but I was damn scared. There was quiet, and it was a deep one, an example is when you can hear it. It is a quiet that pounds in the ears saying you are totally alone and you probably will die. I had to fight terror. If you can't loosen its grip, you might as well throw in the towel. I'd been lucky about two things. The avalanche was not so deep that with a free hand, I could get a pole off my wrist and edge it up through the snow. The other was someone saw me veer off on my own, then the avalanche, then the pole sticking up, and he rescued me. I learned my lesson." He looked at his watch. "He must be open now, so how about some boots for you?"

Mike spoke in a slow way, his tone soft, something I was not used to for Dev talked hurriedly, as if being timed, his voice loud. A good politician's voice. Mike's slow way of talking was probably the result of living in a small mountain town, and time does not press one to hurry. There was little noise to shout above here, except the passing cars on the one main street, and I had the impression even without snow they moved slowly in tune with the less pressured life-style. With effort I set my mind on our immediate goal, to get out of my wet shoes.

Once more he picked me up, carrying me to the threshold of the store. Once more he performed it as a duty, which was just and right because of Laura I would soon meet, who would probably recommend the right things to wear in Truckee, who was probably lighter than I, easier to carry.

As in small towns, Sheriff Montana was a friend of the store owner, an athletic-looking man, younger than both of us. The store owner was Phil. I learned he had been living in Truckee for the past ten years. He'd come to ski and ended up opening a shoe store. He was from the Midwest. He went to the back of the store and brought forth a supply of snow boots. Put away for summer, he said, but, here you never know…

I tried them on, found some black, lightweight nylon boots, and Phil offered us coffee. The boots felt snug and warm, and I wondered how much longer I could have gone on in my sopping sneakers Not long, and the result was I would have been shoeless, therefore confined to my hotel room—or in slippers—to socialize as an observer of a poker game. Instead I found myself in the much more pleasant situation, as a customer in a small store with wide-planked floors, white-washed walls, posters on them of different beautiful seasons, shoes on shelves that spoke of mountain climbing, hiking, and summer flowers and the sweet smell of pines, light rains and pure blue skies. Gratefully I watched Phil put my wet sneakers in a box, slip the whole thing in a bag, my sneaker life in storage for a while. He handed me my receipt.

When we returned to the jeep, I saw the sun had come out, the sky breaking into patterns of solid blue. A snowplow passed by leaving high ridges on either side of the street, and Mike waved to them. We turned onto a side street, and he pulled off and parked.

"Last stop for something warm."

I peered past him at a women's apparel shop. There were summer things in the window. We laughed about it.

"Come on. You can meet Laura."

I had mixed feelings about meeting her; I was curious while at the same time unenthusiastic. Half-right—I was curious, and let's be honest, I didn't want to know her.

A bell tinkled when we entered, and from the back of the narrow shop, watched a young woman approach.

"Laura," Mike said, "I'd like you to meet Margo. This is my daughter," he said to me.

I immediately recognized her from the photo in his office. Her beauty took me more by surprise than the unexpectedness of discovering the name *Laura* was Mike's daughter. She walked with the grace and ease of her father, eyes dark, frankly meeting mine as she approached, yet with a hint of shyness, uncertainty to them. She had the same long, black eyes as her father, the wide, full mouth, the straight nose, her face was fuller than her father's, but her skin pale as his. Her hair was long, thick, and black like Mike's. We shook hands. Hers was a firm handshake. I tried not to stare at this lovely girl, more so than her photograph in his office.

Mike told her what I needed, explaining how Lloyd and I had been held up in the storm, quickly adding, to underline that the circumstances had been proper, he had met us in the hotel on a visit to see Hank and Sally. He and Laura joked about their poker playing interest, their luck in having Lloyd as a guest-player. She offered us coffee, and I laughed, saying I couldn't drink anymore having had about five cups in the last two hours.

"We went to Phil's to buy her some boots," Mike told his daughter. "We had coffee. Earlier we had coffee at the hotel. She's a beginner." He looked at me and smiled, "This is coffee land."

He sat down in one of the two upholstered chairs and picked up a magazine from the table between them.

"Go ahead, ladies. I'll wait quietly."

Laura helped me choose a pair of wool pants and a jacket that were both on sale, dark brown snug pants—the style now—the jacket, a fluffy soft material, brown and turquoise that matched the pants. I picked out a white turtleneck sweater and decided (to myself) that after months of carelessness, I didn't look too bad—or at least there was an improvement, aided by my new hair style. The one I did in the hotel, twisting my lank hair behind my head—one half-step in self-help. The cut of the jacket was short, to the waist, and its fluffiness softened my appearance, gave it character. I would never have thought that a snow outfit could have made me feel good about myself, but it had succeeded. We picked out a knit ski hat that she persuaded me to buy because she claimed it made me look twenty-years-old. I was not exactly convinced of that compliment, but it didn't matter because for that crazy hour, I did feel younger.

I noticed where Mike had been sitting was empty and saw him outside standing in the doorway, watching the street. I had not forgotten the real reason we were detained in Truckee. I wondered if he had noticed something, and with difficulty, I tried to keep my mind on Laura, who was asking me about Salt Lake and Lloyd, our trip. She was eager to hear what we were doing, with an eagerness that I found refreshing, contrary to some young people and a tendency to be self-absorbed. We talked about the shop, and her eyes were lit with pleasure, but then Mike returned, suggesting it was probably time to leave. He put his arm around her protectively and hugged her before we left. Another thought, I was glad to have my checkbook in my purse, it settled next to the glossy page about the rollercoaster.

7.

It was busy. Snow did not hamper the way of life in Truckee. People were dressed accordingly, and the only thing that parents had to give up until the walks were cleared were strollers.

"You have a lovely daughter," I said.

He shook his head, "She's had a hard time of it. I'm thankful she's come out okay. She's in her first year at the university and works part-time at the shop. She likes doing both, and I'm grateful for that."

"It's difficult growing up for most kids," I said. "I've yet to talk to anyone of my own friends who's had a real good time. It's not easy to grow up when one is constantly learning."

He glanced over at me and smiled sadly, "You're right about that. Her mother disappeared when Laura was five."

I stared at the shops, the restaurants as we passed by them, there was one called *The Sierra* whose windows were framed by dark green curtains; I turned my eyes to the windshield and saw the crusts of snow that had accumulated into a half-circle, formed by the sweeping of the wipers. I made a great effort to adjust my mind to what Mike had just pronounced. My whole world had suddenly turned, focused on him. It was whirling, and with extraordinary effort, I tried to stabilize it, tried not to look flustered.

"I'm sorry," I said. "How terrible. It must have been such a suffering for you both…Were there other children?"

"Luckily, or unluckily, no. It might have been good for her to grow up with a sister or a brother. As it went there was just me." Abruptly he changed the subject. "Hey, how about a sandwich? It's close to lunchtime."

He pulled up in front of a diner on a side street. It was a silver railroad car, *Bud's Place* written on the outside.

I was relieved he didn't want to talk about it for the moment. I was too busy eliminating the wrong conclusions I had drawn about his life. Too busy trying to keep in my heart the knowledge that we would soon be leaving Truckee and our lives would move on as they had been doing. How to deal with it.

"This is one of the California Zephyr railroad cars," he said, bringing me back to some sort of a reality. "The inside caught fire years ago, so Bud, the owner, bought it and fixed it up. Was a good decision on his part because it's doing well."

It was crowded and noisy, and the aroma of hamburgers being cooked on a wide iron grill was achingly inviting. It was only 11:30, and I was starved.

"I don't smoke, do you?'

I shook my head, and he led me to the end of the car. We slipped into an original dining-car booth with a large window that once, in its train state, looked out on miles of moving scenery. Bud himself came over and greeted Mike. He was a short thin man with tattoos on his arms to where his sleeves were rolled up. He was kind and asked me if I was from here. I noticed that those in Truckee were interested in outsiders, but after broad questions, they didn't probe. Bud told me he was from New Jersey. He'd lived in Truckee for fifteen years. He had never thought to leave and didn't now. Anyway his wife would hang onto a telephone pole if he did. She loved the Sierras. He took our order for two hamburgers (When he brought them, they were with creamy coleslaw piled high on the plate, fries thin and crisp on the side). I tried to temper myself not to eat greedily for the first bite was delicious—if one could ever say this about a hamburger, mine only a normal experience until then.

"People seem to like it here," I said, thinking also of Phil. "They come and stay."

"They become attached to the small-town atmosphere. We're like one family, but we mind our own business. That's probably where we differ from a small town. Everyone is occupied. They ski, own shops, cater to the tourists, and in the winter, fight the weather. The ones who stay have dealt with the weather and decided they like it. If you've lasted a couple of years of winter, then you'll probably stay." He hesitated, "And…what about you? Are you and Lloyd going to be awhile in Salt Lake?"

"A few days. We both have memories in Salt Lake. He used to live there as a bachelor, and he met my mother there when she was a widow. Then after my sister and I left home and Lloyd retired, they moved to Santa Cruz. That was twenty years ago. It's been three years since she passed away, and we each take turns visiting him. This trip was my idea in hoping to find the right moment to convince him to move—to where my sister lives in Boston, or Washington D.C., my home. But twenty years is a long time to live in one place, it would be hard for him, plus the fact he is stubborn. It would be easier on the East Coast to have him there. Less planning for Santa Cruz," I told him.

There are moments in life—situations—that lend to confessions, to reveal one's past, and for me it was Bud's place, with Mike a stranger, not threatening in judgments, and the noise level was just high enough to interfere with embarrassing intimacy. In that atmosphere, I told him about my decision to leave my husband. It had been necessary to lift this weight from my heart, to face it with someone who didn't know Dev, who barely knew me and would not sympathize. I didn't need sympathy. I just needed to get it all out. I told him we had met before he had left for Vietnam, and when he returned, we married. He had been the only serious attachment in my life. I held nothing back as I told him I had left that marriage two years ago and why. I tried hard to keep control of my emotions for I could feel him keenly listening. His presence across the table was so strong, I felt isolated by it. I was not aware of where we were nor what we were doing here. There was only a person sitting across from me, interested, watching me as I talked.

I finished. I watched some small birds play on a branch of a pine tree. Their wings sprayed the light snow that disappeared in the air. The sky had opened to a clear blue, and the snow everywhere was bright, sparkled in the sun. I had said what I needed. I turned and looked at him.

He had been watching me, his hands clasped lightly together on the table, and he smiled. I smiled back.

"Thank you for listening."

"I had missed Vietnam because of Laura. But I was two years too old to be called anyway. I protested it. I went to Berkeley with a couple of friends from here and took also Laura—she was seven—and marched along with the rest of the protesters. War does things to people. Brings out the best and brings out also the bad. It was an ugly war either way. You and I, we both followed our values. Protesting in Berkeley, however, was less serious than the decision you made."

The song "La Vie en Rose" suddenly filled the diner.

"It's Edith Piaf!" I exclaimed. "Up here. In the Sierra?"

Chuckling he said, "It's the oddity of the diner. Bud got a hold of it in English somewhere and put it in the jukebox for jokes. You'd be surprised how many play it. The big difference from country music makes it *in*. The joke ended being on him. You never know about mountain people," he said.

Piaf's voice rose strong above the noise of the crowd, the romantic words clean in her French accent, "*...when you kiss me heaven sighs...and though I close my eyes...I see La vie en rose...*"

"*Life Is A Rose*, that's the title Bud gave it in the jukebox. Maybe not all the time it is, but we have to believe luck changes, things right themselves."

"Of all the places Lloyd and I could have stopped," I said, "I don't think we would have been as lucky as in Truckee. In its middle, our life is threatened, but the town gives out safe feelings, don't worry it says, like a mother-hen, taking us under her wings. Over a week ago, I was on a Greyhound bus bound for Santa Cruz and now here we are with a car that has followed us on our way to Salt Lake. I don't know what I would have done if you had not been in your office when I was looking for help. Sometimes I think one must relax, let oneself go where life takes you. I like the phrase, *go with the flow...*"

"Yes, it was your luck I was still in my office. Along with that I'm there just twice a week."

"What do you do the rest of the time?"

"Construction. I have my own business. I build cabins for the city folks and houses and whatever else for those who want to stay. It's good work. I've never thought about doing anything else." He stopped. "Salt Lake," he murmured. "Now that you mention it, I almost forgot it was your destination."

"I doubt Lloyd has forgotten," I said. "Either for the reason he would like not to go there anymore and turn around and go home, or now that the sun is out, he is secretly looking forward to the trip. He's never come out and admitted it—Lloyd being Lloyd. I know it's important his going back to the hotel where he used to live. He may want to leave for Salt Lake tomorrow, you know. He's stubborn when he makes up his mind."

"I hope that won't be so. At least give it another day. It'll leave the impression you may be in Truckee a while. In that case, our person may decide to leave. Out of boredom."

"But you don't really think he'll go on, do you, while we're here," I stated dejectedly. "I have the feeling you're being easy on me."

He sighed. "This whole situation is like smoke, Margo. You can't touch it, but it's there. The other side of the coin is I don't want to put you in a state of panic. Unfortunately there is nothing that the police can do since we are dealing with an unknown. The car has even disappeared now. Could be he rented another one, returned the first one. If I were that person, I'd do the same thing. Get rid of the car. If he did this, it was soon after you and Lloyd got installed in the hotel. And he moved fast, since by then he knew where to find you. There are many car rentals around here due to Tahoe. We could check them out, but it would take some time. Could be he'd be using another ID anyway. Let's give it a day more with Santa Cruz. He sure enough has guessed your discovery on being followed. I'm also sure he knows you've come to me. Instead of the pronoun *person*, let's use the masculine. Can't imagine a woman doing all of this. Maybe, you never know." He laughed, "Don't want to underestimate the gifts of a woman."

"But if he got another car, he's pretty well covered, isn't he?" I said. "He's in charge. He knows where we are, but we have no clue as to where he is." It seemed a cold hand had been placed on my back at the thought of it. At the thought of being watched.

"I'm afraid you're right. For now."

"In that case," I said, 'I'd like to get it all over with. Maybe Lloyd and I can sit outside, expose ourselves on a bench somewhere and wait. It'd be better than not knowing."

"Would you be willing to do that? Though not exactly a bench."

I stared at him to see if he was joking. The bright sun that came in the window formed a pattern on my arm. Its warmth made me realize how cold I felt in spite of my new turtle-necked sweater.

"You're serious, aren't you?"

"Yes, I am." Absently I ran my finger along initials that had been carved into the table. "If it's the nephew who murdered the couple, and he's the one following us, I don't remember what he looks like. If he came in now and sat beside us, I wouldn't know him; I wouldn't be able to say, if I saw him walking down the street and Lloyd and I were on a bench, look, he's coming, Lloyd!"

"It doesn't matter," Mike said softly. "You don't have to recognize him. It's important that he knows *you*. And thinks you're alone. The rest leave to him."

"What you're defining is the role of Lloyd and me being open targets," I said, a bit warily and curious.

"That's what I'm thinking," he replied, "because there's no other way. But I could not suggest this to you. It was necessary you defined this yourself. Only you'll be safer than if you and Lloyd struck out on your own to Salt Lake."

Letting those words settle in my mind, he waited. It was crazy, but I felt slightly exhilarated by Mike's words. I seemed to have entered into a third dimension where danger, my feeling of attraction to him, this small town of Truckee tucked in the Sierra, was unreal, and like the sudden snowstorm, it would go its way also. I could do what I wanted because there was no meaning to actions or feelings; I had entered this tiny, existential world to move with it, follow any dangerous path, and pass through unscathed. It brought to mind a pupil in my class who raised his hand and said he still didn't understand the word Existentialism. We had been discussing writers. It turned into a free-for-all of ideas. A reason why I loved teaching.

"Hold me close and hold me fast…the magic spell you cast is La Vie En Rose…" Someone had put money in.

"Tell me what you are thinking," I said.

He didn't look relieved as I thought he might. He frowned.

"First of all, you must believe me that I will not let anything happen to you." He leaned toward me, "You believe that, don't you?"

His face looked strained, eyes so black with earnestness that I had to keep myself from reaching out and touching him. I nodded because I already knew it was so.

He relaxed. "Now I have a question on a whole new subject. Do you ski?"

This I wasn't prepared for. Nor did I have time to weigh what would be in my favor as a reply since I did ski. I had been a good skier when I was in college. But I was not keen to look the fool in deep snow, never having conquered powder skiing, and to be realistic, it had been some time ago.

"The sun is out. How about it? Throw all worries away. It's spring. The lifts stay open until five. It's almost one. We'll be on the hill at two."

"Are you serious?"

"Sure."

"But I haven't skied in years."

"You don't forget. It's like riding a bike. And besides the equipment is better than what you had."

"But clothes!"

"We'll rent what you need up there."

"Oh, Lord," I exclaimed, suddenly remembering, "I forgot to call Lloyd."

"Phone's at the end of the room. If not okay with him, I'll take you back."

"What about you? Your clothes?"

"I keep them in the jeep for decisions like this."

He watched me with amusement, having blocked my last excuse.

"Mike…" I laughed nervously.

"How long has it been?"

"I guess five or six years."

"Only?"

"I'll make a fool of myself."

"No you won't. At least call Lloyd. Maybe you'll have an excuse if it's not fine with him."

Mike gave me the hotel number that he knew by heart. I threaded my way through the crowd that had grown since we came in. A friendly crowd, people nodding, greeting me as if I already knew them. Truckee had welcomed us, and the feeling still emanated from the town. I asked a woman in jeans and a down jacket where the phone was, and she took me by the arm and led me to it.

Edith Piaf had finally given way to country music. Songs I had become familiar with on the car trip while Lloyd slept, for they were entertaining. Words of lost love, looking for it, sorrow at hurting or being hurt, joy…One was about a boy who grew up on a farm, loved his parents, then met a girl, they eloped; he killed her because she was unfaithful and he went to jail, full of guilt because he wronged his mother. Needless to say, a song told a life story.

"Lloyd?" I said when he came to the phone.

"Margo? Where the hell have you been? You've been gone for hours."

"I know. I'm sorry."

"Where are you?"

"I'm in a diner having lunch with Sheriff Montana."

"Well, you should have called earlier. I was worried sick, given our situation. I thought about calling the police."

"I am with the police," I laughed.

"You knew that, but I didn't."

"Lloyd," I began, imagining with relief what the answer would be after his outburst, "Mike suggested he and I go skiing, since the sun came out. But I don't have to," I quickly assured him.

"Shucks, what are you asking me for? Go on."

"But you don't mind? You're there all alone."

"Why should I mind? I *live* alone. Here I've been having a very pleasant time. I've played poker, I've sat in the lobby and had three Cokes while watching the snowfall peter out. and now I'm going to advise Hank on the income tax" (Something Lloyd, accomplished in that field, did for friends in Santa Cruz). "Say," he lowered his voice, "what has Mike decided about the car following us? The tire was changed, so does he think it's safe to leave for Salt Lake tomorrow?"

"No, he doesn't," I said with firmness in my voice in case of resistance. "At least not tomorrow. I hope that's alright with you," in a tone that it better be.

"I can put up with another day," he said. "Hank and Sally are good people."

I was now destined to go skiing but thankful that Lloyd was in a good humor.

"I'll see you in a few hours, Lloyd."

"Take your time, and don't break a leg."

8.

IN SKI COUNTRY, THE DISTANCE TO THE TOP OF THE SLOPE CAN BE far, but in well-organized resorts, it doesn't take long to get there, nor to rent equipment. We had driven the ten miles to Squaw Valley, rented clothes and equipment for me, then taken the main cable car to the chair lifts, all in an hour. We carried our skis to a flat area, slipped them on, and I followed Mike to one of the lifts. The sky was clear now. and the light reflecting off the snow was blinding. I was glad I had listened to Mike's insistence on investing in goggles instead of relying on my sun glasses; the snow was feathery, layered light as dust, brilliant, sparkling in the sun. Soon this would be packed down, but now it was virgin, free and breathing, sorry to be touched. Slipping ahead on our skis toward the lift, they rippled through it free and easily, white particles falling aside effortlessly, forming delicate ridges along the path we made. Because it had been a surprise snowfall, there were not many skiers as we rode up, and the almost empty chair lift rattled and thumped in its emptiness as if out of sorts for that reason. In the distance, you could hear whoops of joy from those who thrilled skiing in the deep snow. I was not feeling that carefree. In my skiing days, I always avoided deep snow, never having learned how to handle it, nor wanting to, and my enthusiasm had not come now with so many years of not learning. What's more, in descending, I was gasping for air, the altitude another factor that I was not used to. The oxygen entered my lungs in stingy little handfuls, thin and anemic, in no mood to be generous.

Mike stopped and turned. I was lagging far behind.

"Everything okay?"

"I'm glad I bought the goggles," I confessed, calling down to him. "For the rest, I've never been a good deep snow skier." That was all I could get out of me before gasping for another handful of air.

"We'll take it slow."

He waited for me until I came alongside of him. He was resting back on his poles, looking up at the mountains.

"Today is a gift. All this snow, sun, no crowds," he said. "Sometimes I'd thought of taking Laura and leaving here when she was young, then I'd come up and ski, get close to it all, breathe in the air, and wonder how I could have had such a thought. God, I love the mountains."

He had stopped in the shadow of a pine tree.

"I envy you," I said. "I've never felt that strongly about a place. I imagine this is what comes from living where your parents did."

"My Indian blood probably has a lot to do with it. I inherited that feeling of being close to the land."

"But *Montana* doesn't sound Indian."

"Nick Montana was my father. He was Italian. He came over when a kid with his family. For a while, they lived in New York, then moved West when construction jobs opened up on the railroads, a life-saver for a lot of the emigrants. From Sacramento they moved on to working on the railroad in the Sierras. Later my grandfather earned enough money to open a small grocery store in Truckee—which was where my father spent the rest of his life. He met my mother here. She was from one of the few Indian tribes left in the area. The Indians used to trade at the store. My father liked to tell us how my mother would come in with her family, and he and she would talk while her family traded—they had the skins and baskets, my grandfather had the sugar and salt. Little did my father care about that," Mike laughed, "because as he told it, he was impressed by the beauty of this girl who ended up being my mother.

"When my grandfather died, my father continued with the store—the same one where Laura works. I didn't want to lose it after my parents died, so

I kept it and re-modeled it, found someone to run it. As it turned out, with Laura now old enough, she's learned a lot in managing it herself. I'm sorry Dad and Mom didn't live to see this. They lost their lives in a car accident ten years ago. A matter of being in the wrong place at the wrong time. It was a well-traveled road, but it was spring, and the snow had loosened up above. I like to think it was *they* who saved me when I was later in that avalanche."

"How tragic," I said.

"Yes, for me…both of them at once. But that's the Sierra: Beautiful and always unpredictable. In their case, sympathetic because they died in each other's arms. At least that. So I never left. I don't know if not being able to leave a place is good or bad," he said, rummaging through his pockets. He found what he was looking for, "Here's some cream. Maybe put some on your face before we go up again. This sun can be nasty."

He held my goggles and watched me put the cream on.

He looked concerned. "It's not real strong cream. You'll have to keep applying it."

"I'll shade my face with my hands on the lift," I said.

Suddenly he slipped a glove off, reached over, and touched my face.

"You're very fair," he said. He cupped my chin and ran his thumb gently across my cheeks, and my legs went weak.

He leaned down and kissed me softly, and I responded until light snow showered us from a branch where a bird had rested.

Mike looked up. "A crow. Look at it go!"

The bird was flapping hard to gain altitude. We watched it pump, cruise, pump once more, then satisfied with its altitude, it sailed into the distance.

He laughed. "It's off and not too happy about the snow. The snow's spoiled all its resting places."

He took the tube from my hand and applied cream to my face, in less the gentle way as before but dutifully, the moment of intimacy having disappeared. Both of us were new at this, or at least I was, but I sensed he felt awkward also. How does one begin again? How do I? How do I read the other person and on a ski hill—as such, I did not know how. I could not imagine myself with another man; the thought never occurred to me in the scenario of my leaving Dev. Only now…So what was a kiss? Except that my legs continued to be weak from it as we finished our descent and slipped forward once more to the lifts. Thoughts were going through my mind as I tried to make light conversation.

"What do they eat so high up here?"

"Who?"

"The crows."

"Oh, the crows…" He laughed. We both laughed self-consciously.

"They rob nests," he said. "And garbage, which is probably easier to find. They keep the place clean but I've never liked the idea of a carnivorous bird."

"Their cries are lonely," I said. "In Washington, when it rains, they line up on the telephone wires. They don't look happy."

After that we continued in silence. I felt ill-at-ease. What was he thinking? Had I responded too eagerly? Had his gesture been just spontaneous and he had already forgotten? Was he thinking about the crows?

We arrived at the lift, and the lift-keeper strolled over to us. He could afford to do that as no one else was in line. He and Mike had a friendly conversation, he glancing at me with curiosity as they talked.

"I think he was wondering who I was," I said as we swung off the platform.

"It's not often I'm seen alone with an out-of-town woman. Speaking of that, I've been thinking about a plan to bring up with you and Lloyd."

"A plan? You've found one already?"

He laughed. "While you were clothes shopping with Laura. Are you ready?"

"Go ahead."

The kiss had drifted off on the wings of the bird, as if it hadn't happened, the real world opening before us on the lift.

"You and Lloyd have decided to play the slot machines and have lunch. There's a big casino not far from the hotel with a good restaurant and full of slot machines. Very popular. Noisy with a lot of people. Most of all close by, so he won't have to go far for him to follow you—or losing you and ruining our plan. You're safe there among people, our man is happy because he blends in. We'll flush him out. I'll follow you in a rented car—my jeep too obvious. I'll blend into the crowd also, but you'll never be out of my sight. What is more, you'll be covered by the police."

"How will he know where we'll be?"

"He's followed you this far. He's not going to give up now. Once you and Lloyd are in the casino, you go to the slots. Set your purse down within reach but not that close either. Then you get busy with the slots." He looked over at me smiling, "Maybe you'll win a jackpot. But not on that one as it will be fixed before you arrive. It will have a number on it for you to see. Lloyd will use the one next to you."

"Is this what is called a *sting?*"

"If it all goes as planned, yes."

"I think Lloyd should stay here. I'll go by myself."

"I don't think you can do that, Margo. Being alone will look like a set-up—which it is."

"Let's leave it at this point for now. We'll talk to Lloyd, and I will call Santa Cruz for the latest developments."

The lift passed alongside a creek, almost hidden because of the high mound of snow bordering it, but the sun found a low, tender spot and made it sparkle. Towards the end, we began a steep climb. I looked back. Lake Tahoe lay flat and shimmering in the valley below, a sheet of dark blue, as part of a land that had been scrubbed and shined; the forest met its edges, framed it, then backed off in all directions, clusters and clusters of dark green pines.

"A contribution from the Sierra," said Mike. "You're looking at enough water to cover the entire state of California to a depth of over a foot—ironical when you think how dry this state is—whoa, prepare to land."

I turned and saw the end of the lift looming ahead. We gathered our poles, slipped onto the lift platform, then down around it to the crest of the hill. Below we could still see the lake, calm and still, parts of it almost black in the shadows, the trees surrounding it clearly outlined in the pure air. The few skiers who had gone ahead of us had left neat, deep tracks from their descent, and aside from their tracks, the snow was unruffled, uniform, on a hill steeper than I would have wished. I followed Mike down, who took slow, wide turns for my sake, a good, confident skier, and on similar days would have been one of those whooping for joy while cutting a clean path in its newness.

I fell.

He stopped and shouted up to me, "Shift the weight, Margo. In deep snow, the upper one carries all of it. One, then the other as you go down. Helps if you say it as you go."

I got up, started, my skis crossed, I fell. I got up once more, and each time Mike kept moving farther down the hill leading me on. But the time I got down the hill, I had made some decent turns without falling. I stood there panting.

"Are you tired?"

"No," I lied.

"Up we go again," Mike said. "You're getting the hang of it. You can rest on the lift. Your legs shaking?"

I laughed the question off, determined to be game, not to let him see how tired I was. The fatigue was there, serious from the experience of the past happenings and now trying to look decent on a pair of skis in deep snow after so many years.

On the lift, Mike rehearsed the plan once more. I began to nourish the peculiar feeling of adventure where danger seemed far from it.

The sun was melting the snow on the tree branches, and fine strands of ice were forming, lengthening with the afternoon to thin as needles. After various descents, I had gotten the hang of handling the deep snow, thanks to pride, along with Mike's coaching that was kind and patient and merited progress in his student.

He promoted me later to a longer trail, another lift, and for the first time I was able to experience a fraction of the excitement—that my new ability allowed—of breaking new snow, skis shifting, the powder blowing back into my face.

"Tomorrow it'll be heavy," he said. "It's too late in the year for the good snow to stay."

We were on the hill going up for one last run. It had turned cool, the spring sun backing off, and I didn't want to return too late because of Lloyd. Already I felt as if I had deserted him, even though the tone of his voice indicated differently.

We watched a lone skier on the steeper side of the lift break a trail from the crest. He cut a nice figure, an expert skier in a tight-fitting orange and black ski outfit, his tracks the only disturbance in the smooth swell of white. This I had been thinking as we heard the rumble and suddenly appeared a wave of white on his track. It happened so fast, the noise, the wave—a stretch of the Pacific Ocean, a tongue curling and growing—that it stunned us into momentary silence. The skier disappeared under a blanket of snow and with that, as the lift drew our chair even to his fall, Mike threw out his pole, it ending as a spear, slanted, the handle barely showing against the whiteness not far from where the skier had disappeared. Instinctively he lifted the guard rail to jump down but thought better of it because of the chasm directly below us. The only lucky break was we were not far from the end of the lift.

"Count the lift gates!" Mike said.

We both counted three, then sat in rigid silence until we slid up onto the platform and Mike disappeared down the hill.

"There's been an avalanche," I yelled to the lift keeper, who was standing in the sun next to the lift house. "Someone's under it," I gasped.

He stopped the lift, slipped on his skis, grabbed what looked like snow shoes, and in what seemed ten seconds, was beside me.

"Where?"

"Three gates down. On the right. My friend just skied down to help."

"Got you," over his shoulder as he sailed off, myself relieved not asked to lead the way.

I would like to say I had never skied so well going those three gates down the hill, but it was only luck that had kept me from falling, keeping me upright on that steeper side. Scenes of Mike's parents buried by an avalanche in their car flashed through my mind, Mike himself, had he now been sucked into it as quicksand?

When I reached the spot, Mike and the lift keeper were digging furiously, using the snowshoes as shovels the lift keeper took with him.

"Go on down," Mike yelled, "and tell them there's no one at the lift station!"

That was all he said. They were waist deep in snow, flinging it aside with snowshoes. I thought I saw the head of the skier before I left, vaguely heard Mike and the lift keeper gasping for breath.

I crossed over under the lift to the side we had been skiing on and forced myself to take my time, make calm turns so I wouldn't fall; it was still a long way to the end, and the snow was becoming crusty with the drop in temperature. Midway, and what seemed forever, I stopped to catch my breath, looked up, and made out Mike, along with the lift keeper—and surely it could not be true, but it was, the rescued skier coming down the hill.

I stared, I laughed. Soon I would wake up for all this was a dream: the elderly couple would still be treasure hunting, the tire of Lloyd's car had not been slashed, nor had there been a snowstorm, therefore nothing would prevent Lloyd and me from being on our way soon, or perhaps I was still on the Greyhound bus going from the airport to Santa Cruz. I could take my pick from one of them.

Were these the mystic ways of the Sierra? Where normalcy of life was returned with the same suddenness it seemed to have been taken? Where with great white sweeps she reached and lowered to settle dispassionately, peacefully over a victim. Then took time to allow freedom, or not, as she saw fit? She had whims.

I watched them ski down. The skier in orange and black looked expert as before the avalanche. He and the lift keeper shot past me. Mike pulled up opposite me, grinning.

"We got the best of our mountain this time," he said, taking his glove off and brushing the snow from his hair, "his skis came off and he ended up in a crouching position, so that made a little breathing space for him. Another minute though and my pole would've slipped down in the snow with a hard time finding him."

"She changed her mind," I said. "We went by on the lift, and she changed her mind so you *could* find him. She plays with us."

I surprised myself at this spiritual interpretation.

Leaning forward on his poles, he looked at me laughing, "I believe you have a point there."

I should have known my observation was not so original because he, man of the mountains with an Indian background, already knew this.

"I suppose I have just given her a soul," I said, the novice.

I could not look away from him. His black eyes held me, and only a Sierra avalanche could have released me from his look. He slipped toward me, opening his skis just enough so that mine fit between them, and he could take me in his arms.

And if the mountain had planned this also, then she had a good heart. She was one who sympathized, understood, knew that I could not have gone on much longer without this man holding me, kissing me as he was. And, yea, she was my friend.

We said nothing as we pulled away from each other. The air had turned dry and icy with the lowering sun, a reddish sun that had now filled the long icicles hanging from the fir trees, so they glistened orange, a feisty spring sun that had burrowed into the winding grooves of ski tracks putting light into them and left hard, dark shadows under the swooping pine branches. The lift chairs hung motionless, and around us was a heavy stillness, a hush, likened to the room of a sleeping child broken only by the scraping of our own skis as we finished our descent on what now had become a roughened, icy slope. Magic followed me on our descent.

I stopped for a moment and watched Mike ski down. I had been so involved in my own performance that I hadn't turned full attention to his own ability. He was an expert, short, quick turns, and not surprising for one who had lived a life in the mountains. But there was more to it, there was his grace, his being one with the mountain, his spirit of freedom and independence that showed. This was his world, his past, that of his ancestors, and I was the observer.

He stopped and turned and raised his arm to me, then continued. He did not look back.

On our return, Mike gave a ride to a friend from Truckee. Next to Mike, I set my head back against the seat and let their conversation pass over me. My thoughts went to the murdered elderly couple in Santa Cruz, the carefully settled snow from a mountain over its deed—the causes from nowhere, unknown, normalcy once more, that even for me, Mike also, was unreal and it would pass.

The only thing I remember before falling asleep was his hand, its warmth, that had reached over to cover mine.

9.

When we entered the hotel, I found Lloyd sitting in the comfortable living-room lobby, and from the way he was facing the door, knew he was waiting for us. I thought to myself that I shouldn't have left him the whole day. It was one thing to enjoy new friends like Hank and Sally, play poker, but inevitable, the Nelsons had their hotel responsibilities and could not spend the entire day entertaining Lloyd. And Lloyd without a Coke as he was then looked even more lonely. Seeing him like that recalled the mission I had brought with me regarding the retirement home. Had it been a hundred years since then? Fifty since he had told me about Junie? Now both subjects had lost importance, taken on smaller dimensions.

His face lit up when he saw us. "Well, well, how'd it go?"

"Wonderful. I learned to ski in the deep snow. But then I had a good teacher."

"Hi, Lloyd." Mike came up alongside of me. He stood and looked down at Lloyd apologetically, "I kept her out all day, didn't I?" a tone of contrition in his voice. "You got along okay?"

"If you call winning $10 in poker a good day, then I had a good day. And if you want to know the truth, I wasn't lying earlier when I said I liked the snow. It's been a long time since I've seen so damn much of it." Then he was quiet, looked down at his hands folded in his lap. He looked up, his face serious, "I think you better check your room, Margo. Right now."

I had an ugly premonition.

"I think someone's been in there." I felt a surge of ice in my bones.

"What are you talking about, Lloyd?"

"Well, I'd gone up some hours ago, and as I got out of the elevator, I saw a guy walking down the hall, away from me, toward the staircase. I had a feeling. I went to my room, and the door was locked, so I don't think anyone came in. Also, because when I opened it. I had a shirt hanging from the doorknob in the bathroom and it was as I left it. Anyway there was nothing out of place, and the cleaning girl had already been there—bed was made. I tried your door, and it wasn't locked. I didn't go in. I decided to wait until you came back. To tell the truth, I guess I didn't want to know."

"Maybe the girl who cleans the room left it open," I said without conviction because I then remembered the room had been tended to while we were at breakfast. And I locked the door after that when I left. I remembered clearly locking the door because the key got stuck for a moment and I had to work with it to get it out.

"Lloyd, did you tell the Nelsons?"

"Oh, what the hell. They had gotten busy, and I didn't want to go downstairs and bother them. The guy had gone anyway. There wasn't a thing I could do, or they could do, until you got back."

"And you've been sitting here all this time waiting for us?" I exclaimed, dismay in my voice.

"You're damn right, and you've come back none too soon," he said laughing, seriousness leaving his face.

Mike pulled up a chair next to Lloyd and sat down. "Can you remember what he looked like, Lloyd? Anything at all?"

"I knew that would be the first question, and I wish I could. He was at the end of the hall, his back to me, and all I saw, or remember, was a heavy coat, and from the back it looked like he had a scarf around his neck. He disappeared so fast."

I took a deep breath because it seemed my breathing had altogether ceased while listening to it all.

"Can you remember anything about the coat?" Mike said.

"Only one thing. It looked like tweed. Don't ask me why that sticks in my mind because I can't tell you."

"Do you remember if he was wearing a hat?"

"I think it was a hat. A brimmed hat of some kind."

"Anything else you can remember?"

"That's about all I can do for you two," Lloyd said. "The older I get, the more I remember what happened forty years ago, but I'll damned if I can remember much about what happened yesterday. Or a few hours ago."

"You did great," Montana said. "How about us going up to the room—your room, Margo. We'll do that before mentioning this to the Nelsons. In case of a false alarm."

We took the elevator up. The hallway was quiet and empty, as it had been earlier, but now there was an eeriness to it. I reached out to turn the handle of the door. As Lloyd said, it was open.

I have never experienced robbery, but by others' recounts, there has always been the feeling of something amiss, even when at the outset things seem in order. *Electrical currents…an unnatural quiet in the air…*was what a friend who had been robbed had described. So it was with me.

At the outset, things seemed to be in place. My bed had been made up and clean towels in the bathroom. But there was the same eeriness to it as in the hallway. Then I noticed some of the clothes I had hung up were now over the back of a chair. My cosmetic case was not in the bathroom but beside the bed, where he had probably sat to go through it. I opened my suitcase that sat on the luggage stand. It had been gone through, belongings topsy-turvy. I was dumbfounded. Then angry. Angry that a robber's hands touched my personal items, worse a hand surely of a murderer. I wondered how I could have felt so cocky, adventurous some time ago when Montana talked about laying a trap for whoever this was.

"Well, I'll be damned," Lloyd said.

Lloyd and I both walked over and sat on the bed. Somehow I got there, though I don't remember taking the steps.

"What now?" Lloyd watched Mike coming back from the bathroom with a glass of water. The fact that Lloyd could find his voice made me realize I had to get a grip on myself, Lloyd, old therefore fragile, was showing more spunk than I these moments. But for me the day had been long, I hardly remembered when the first adventure, or emotional experience, and begun in the past ten hours. What's more he had not been the person whose room had been entered. The word *transgression* took on another role that now was added to the car and murder of the couple in Santa Cruz.

Mike handed me the glass of water, "Lloyd, are you positive no one entered your room?"

"Yes. Except of course the girl who cleaned the room."

"Suitcase in order?"

"I checked it, and it was fine."

"Mike," I said, "we haven't even talked about my being robbed. What was taken." The glass of water had helped, and I got up and started going through my belongings.

"I'll wager you won't find anything missing," said Montana. "He didn't follow you all the way from Santa Cruz to rob you in Truckee. For that matter, he could have robbed you in Santa Cruz"—he stopped a moment. "So why didn't he then?" he wondered thoughtfully.

I had found nothing missing after I checked. Montana was right. It seemed the person was looking for something. At least it took the weight from his out-and-out wanting to kill us. I felt also a sense of relief: if we had something he wanted, then maybe our living was important. I sat back down on the bed beside Lloyd, and we were quiet for a moment, the three of us thinking.

"One thing interesting," Mike said, "is that he was careful about going through your things. This is a neat person. People on drugs are not necessarily neat."

"If you don't mind me adding my two bits," Lloyd said finally, "I think he's looking for something that has to do with the couple. Or Minnie, the sister, even. What else could it be?"

Mike was walking up and down the room. He unzipped his ski jacket and took it off.

"Let's go over the visit. When you entered to see the apartment. When you met the couple for the first time."

"The whole place was depressing, that's what I remember. Your mother would never have wanted to live there. Too dark. Even the rug was depressing. I don't know what got into me. I just don't," he said looking over at me.

"Lloyd," I said, "for about fifteen minutes you just wanted to change a little bit of your life. That's all." Wondering about myself and my fifteen minutes of hope somewhere today when with Mike. A man in tune to his own world. A man who had lost his wife—that part I would be going against family norms, my own mother—heaven help me—her straight-laced Irish-Catholic upbringing. There were forces around putting up stop signs, telling me if I did not heed them, there would be bad trade-offs. I would be punished.

"Margo," Montana interrupted my thoughts, "between your and Lloyd's visit to the apartment downstairs and the time you left Santa Cruz, you must have acquired something. Think. Now you didn't see them again, right? After that visit?"

"No, definitely not," I said.

"When did you and Lloyd leave town after that?"

I looked at Lloyd. "Three or four days later, wasn't it?"

"I think so. Shucks, I can't remember."

"So," Montana said, "during those four days, you acquired what he is now looking for. Because you didn't see them again, it had to be during the time you and Lloyd went to see the apartment—how am I doing?" he laughed. "Slowly we'll get to the bottom of it."

"We brought you a problem, didn't we?" I said disconsolately.

Mike went over and stood in front of us. "This is my job," he said quietly, then held his eyes on mine, "and I'm glad you turned off at Truckee. So let's go on. Let's go back once more to when you walked into the apartment of Minnie."

Lloyd and I went over it again, the room filled with dolls and furniture, the heavy drapes, the nephew on the couch—whom we had already tried to remember more accurately a hundred times—how talkative the elderly couple was, what they talked about, which was looking for the sister's will, how she liked to play the game of treasure hunt, and that their father had engineered the roller coaster on the boardwalk.

"Let's go back to the will once more," Mike said, "to remember anything else."

I wracked my brain. "To be honest," I said, "at a certain point, I was thinking of only one thing: how to leave, and gracefully, in light of the sister's death."

"All I remember," Lloyd said, "was after they started on the boardwalk bit, I was ready to walk out the front door. Your mother and I know people like that, Margo, who'll talk an arm and a leg off of you. The only thing to do is to leave." He added, "That was the way I felt then, but what we know now… they were kind-hearted people."

I looked at Lloyd. "The information on the history of the boardwalk that they handed me just before leaving! When they brought me the information, they brought also a purple envelope that was with it. Both were in a kitchen drawer. Minnie's brother was very excited because the word *hunt* was written on the envelope. He said she used colored envelopes for her treasure hunts and thought the purple envelope would be the beginning of this one. Could be I recall this now because at the time it seemed a good idea to use colored envelopes, so they could be seen—for a treasure hunt—my vague thought Minnie seemed organized. Her brother was sure she had hidden all her money and then the envelope turned up. You and I left on that note because the whole idea seemed far-fetched, but they could hardly wait to get started."

"Now that you mention it, I do remember," Lloyd said. "It didn't make sense to me except a woman who had dolls all over the house and a big picture of a treasure chest on the wall next to a big cuckoo clock could do something like that—a purple envelope with the word "hunt" on it. So now what?"

The three of us were silent. I had a feeling that Mike was patiently letting us talk, figuring things out. An interruption would stop any train of thought.

My mind was now moving on. My purse had always been with me, even while skiing—in the sense I had checked it in a locker with my new boots, and after skiing, took them both from the locker again. It contained my checkbook and not a thought ever to leave it alone in my room. Now it was still on my shoulder as I sat on the bed. I pulled it in front of me. It was the link. We all knew it in our anxious silence as I quickly unzipped one side. I fumbled with the opening. There were two: One for the money and keys, urgent items. The other for the less needy things, and I knew I had automatically slipped the roller coaster sheet of information there to read once I had returned home. Frame it. Moreover I probably wouldn't have noticed it in the compartment anyway because, being thin and slick, it was plastered against the inside. I felt around for it, catching a finger on the page, pulled it out.

I stared at the front of the page. There was a photograph of the boardwalk, the main buildings with their onion-styled cupolas, the roller coaster itself looming behind it like the hump of a snake. Below the picture was a long paragraph on the history of the roller coaster. Mike had seated himself on the bed next to me.

"Look," he pointed to the bottom of the paragraph where there was a small arrow made from a ballpoint pen and indicated turning the page. There, on the flip side, were boardwalk descriptions, a photo of people strolling in front of concessions, kids eating cotton candy. But at the bottom there were letters, each precisely underlined so as not to make a mistake with the one next to it, they making all one word.

"Who's got a pen?" Mike jumped up, instinctively pat his ski sweater where one of course wasn't. I opened the drawer of one of the side tables and found a hotel postcard, no pen,

Lloyd said, "I've got one," and reached inside his coat jacket pocket.

Mike read the letters to me. I wrote them down on the postcard.

"Okay, let's see what we have here," he said.

"Ten letters. They all run together," I said, then seeing it wasn't so difficult, *closetwall* became *closet wall*. I held the separated word up for them to see.

"Well, now I've heard everything, Lloyd said. "I've heard a lot of crazy things in life, but this takes the cake."

"This was the end of her treasure hunt—the closet," I said, hardly believing it myself. "Then he was after my purse. The nephew was sitting there watching them hand the information on the roller coaster to me. He saw me put it in my purse, he heard me say I'd keep it there…but how could he have known about the message on it?"

Mike said, "From what you told me, they had just found one colored envelope while you were there. The purple one. Had to be the beginning of the hunt because it had the word 'hunt' on it. That envelope led to the others until they learned the place the treasure was to be found, which was in your purse."

"In that case," I said, "why didn't they come up and ask me for it?"

"Because," Mike said, "could be they were dead. The murderer saw your suitcases, followed you on the highway to here."

Lloyd and I were stunned into silence.

"I thank God your mother wasn't around for this," he finally said.

"So he killed them…" I barely heard myself pronouncing the words. Suspecting is one thing; now the reality was numbing. The fact that Lloyd and I had walked in on someone who was mulling over a way to kill two people…

"And one of them was his uncle!" Lloyd said incredulously, "People whom we had innocently been talking with…"

"Worse things than this have happened in the world of drugs, Lloyd," Mike said, "and I suspect it was drug related. Ego's everything in the drug world. Family, loved ones…they're only obstacles. Noting matters except the need…"

His voice trailed off. He got up and went to the window. He stood with his back to us looking out. A gloomy pall fell over the room. Lloyd and I sat waiting for Montana to come back. For a moment, he had distanced himself from us, slipped into his own world, and I felt a heaviness in my heart that had nothing to do with the murder of the elderly couple or even my own worries.

"Mike," I called softly. Lloyd gave me a glance of curiosity. What I wanted to do was go over to Montana, embrace him, rest my head against his back until whatever he felt had passed. Would I have done this if we were alone? Would a kiss in the snow be enough to allow me to comfort him now? I was grateful Lloyd was there for I would not have known what to do.

Lloyd broke into the gloom; he seemed to have been thinking of other things and not noticed Mike's melancholy.

"Margo, I think we ought to call Junie. She lives right there."

I said, "I don't know if that's a good idea at this point, Lloyd."

The sadness that enveloped Mike seemed to have passed as he came over and quietly switched on the table lamp beside the bed. The sudden light made me blink in the room that had filled with evening twilight that none of us had noticed.

"Margo is right," he said gently to Lloyd. "No one else for the present. First and foremost, I've got to call the detective in Santa Cruz."

"But why would he kill them, Mike?" Lloyd said.

"It'd be clear if we knew what the last envelope said. Now we can only guess. My guess is it said *what* was hidden—and *where* it was, which was on the page Margo had in her purse. I'm not so sure it was a will. The nephew or anyone, wouldn't kill for a will. That wouldn't make sense, even to a drug addict. It could only be her money hidden there. But how much? Ten dollars or money for a lifetime? The killer took a chance on that one—do away with them and find the answer in Margo's purse. A desperate try."

Mike went over and picked up the phone. We listened to him give the number of the police in Santa Cruz, indicating the charge was an official call. We were quiet until the call came through, then his recounting what we had found in my purse and the word *closet wall*.

I was sorry not to have the excuse to call Junie. Because she and our mother had been close friends. I had spent time with both of them together on my visits. I would have appreciated her feminine companionship right now also. I am sure that comfort is what Lloyd had in mind also.

"Well, we won't know anything until they check the closet. That's what they're going to do now. Detective Hare is going to call me back as soon as they do. We'll sit tight."

In the meantime, Montana told Lloyd about the plan of our going to the casino. Nothing changed in that respect. The breaking into my room and the information I had in my purse only made what we had to do more urgent. If this was not done, our safety would always be the air and a killer would not be caught.

"This is a hell of a note, that's all I can say. It's a darn pity, damn sickening, these drugs. I've seen it for so long in Santa Cruz, and now it comes knocking right here at our door. Margo," he looked over at me, "I'm sorry you had to come right now. I feel it's my fault."

"If you look at things that way, Lloyd," Mike said, "and Margo hadn't come, you might've gone down to see the apartment anyway and ended up with the information in *your* pocket. An eighty-three-year-old sitting duck who was all alone. To me that doesn't sound so good."

Montana had a teasing way with Lloyd, and Lloyd enjoyed it.

"I'd probably be a *dead* duck," Lloyd laughed.

Looking at him very seriously, I said, "Lloyd, I'm going to go alone to the casino. I want you to stay here. I'm fine alone."

He interrupted, along with a hard look, "You're doing nothing of the kind. I don't want to hear one more word about it."

I backed off. That settled it.

Suddenly the phone rang. Mike answered it, and we waited, watching him intently as he listened.

"Jesus!" he exclaimed. "Tell me again!"

Phone to his ear, he spun around and looked at us.

"What the hell?" Lloyd looked at me questioningly.

Mike made a gesture for something to write on. I handed him the postcard. He scribbled on it: *Found money. Two thousand dollars.*

I read it, then handed it to Lloyd.

We sat dumbfounded as we listened to Mike's conversation with Detective Hare. *Dumfounded* now become a common word. Questions and answers went back and forth, from Mike's side all the information that Lloyd and I had—our description of the nephew (that entered into the twilight zone of lost counts). Finally Mike went into the plan about the casino. Conversation indicated the police were going to be sent from Santa Cruz to cover us there. As I listened, it seemed incredible that Lloyd and I were in the middle of this thing. That it was even happening at all.

Montana finally hung up.

"The money was in a shoe bag attached to the closet wall behind her clothes. Each place held a shoe, except the one in the middle. In that one was $2,000 cash and a note saying where her bank was. The cash was household spending money—all in one-hundred-dollar bills. The bank was Bank of America, just up the street, where she could go anytime and draw on two and a half million dollars at 3 percent interest. There pay her bills, bring back money for the shoe pocket, and what she needed for daily living." He shook his head in disbelief. "So that's it: a murder for *$2,000.*

"Only one envelope was found—one the policemen came across, it rolled in a ball on the kitchen counter. Blue. It was left there until I called about the piece on the roller coaster that Margo had in her purse. In the rolled-up envelope, it said the last one was taped under the dining room table. So it was *that* one, the one under the table, that had written on it to go to the piece on the roller coaster for the final answer—where the treasure was, therefore we return again to Margo's purse. The killer probably stuffed the one under the table in his pocket, killed the couple, then went off to find Margo—or her purse. Probably by that time it had been well figured out by the killer that the treasure meant life's savings and quite a bit—if not all—in hidden cash. That goes back to the conversation you both had with the brother when you were there, he convinced she had no will. A big incentive for someone capable to kill for a lot of money. So he followed you both. He was pretty sure Margo wouldn't be far from her purse and the final clue to the location of the treasure. The tire was slashed to keep you there. He searched your room today, Margo, the obvious hope you might have left it there: you gone, Lloyd playing cards. Was a risk for him—as a matter-of-fact Lloyd saw him—but I imagine by that time he was pretty obsessed. After all he had killed two people, so he couldn't run back now. How he found the room number is a kind of mystery. Could be he called the hotel pretending to be a friend and whoever was at the desk gave him the number. We're a small town and trust people."

"Well, I never thought I'd live long enough to say I've not only heard everything but seen everything, and it's both," Lloyd said. "The joke was on us because we thought she had a fortune hidden. Maybe not a wrong guess considering the way she decorated her home. I for one didn't doubt it. She was a smart lady. One thing I don't get is how did he know when we were leaving Santa Cruz? Or even that we *were* leaving?"

Mike sat down in one of the Victorian chairs, too small for him he got up again, "I was thinking about that, too. Obviously he was keeping an eye on you. Maybe he saw suitcases, something that indicated you were going out of town—do you leave a note for the post office for example?"

Lloyd said, "He must've seen the envelope I left for the post office. We always leave one for the postman when going out of town. It couldn't be missed; it's sticking out, so he'll see it."

"But how would he have figured to get back in the house once he had the information about where the money was? Police always ribbon off places of crime," I said.

"Could be he simply hadn't thought that far ahead—too greedy to be careful, or in some sort of a way, he knew how to get into the house assuming it empty. Who knows?" Montana said. "He could have studied that while visiting his uncle. If it was the nephew."

"Oh, those shoe bags," Lloyd said. "One was in my closet when I lived at the Hotel Utah. Worthless. I never could find the shoe in it that I was looking for, then a tug of war to pull it out. Finally gave up and never used the thing. But as a private bank—not a bad idea."

The three of us laughed.

Mike put on his ski jacket. "I'm going downstairs to talk to Hank and Sally. They should know about someone entering your room. They can't do anything about it except worry and be sorry, but they should know. They may be able to throw some light on it. I'll invite myself to dinner," he said over his shoulder as he exited out the door.

10.

DINNER THAT EVENING WAS SPENT WITH SALLY AND HANK NELSON in their living quarters. Spacious and comfortable around their dining room table. Moreover private, as there were plans to go over on what would take place the next day. Hank and Sally now fully informed, regarding the double murder in Santa Cruz. The importance of my purse and what it contained.

Over entry into my room, they had not enough words of sorrow. It assumed someone had called the desk, a friend, and the girl gave the room number.

"The voice of a murderer could sound like any other," Hank grimly concluded, "and, with the room number, anyone good at lock-picking could open a door." Added information, Sally's permission to the cleaning girl, if finished early, could go skiing. Therefore, according to when Lloyd saw the man, the rooms had been cleaned the girl gone.

I did not bring up if Lloyd had surprised someone on the empty floor picking my lock. No need to ask him. I knew the answer, "...your mother would have had company."

Around the table, plans were finalized for the next morning. Mike, to drive Hanks's car, his own now recognized; Lloyd and myself following, he driving his car with new tire. Destination: Casino. Tahoe.

"I'm getting a slight feel of what actors go through," I said.

"But the audience is different," said Sheriff Montana half seriously.

Sheriff Montana: The title around me invisible, like a soft protection, and in my mind, I used it.

Hank and Sally were suddenly called back to duties, and Lloyd left us to retire. Alone at the dinner table, we made light conversation, an awkwardness to it. Our afternoon hours ago overtaken by tomorrow, the necessity of Lloyd and myself in keeping our wits together. I was thankful that tonight my mind was on tomorrow and our plans and what would happen and my trying not to be fearful, although I was. Lloyd and his age—this was not for him. I would deal with the pain of a lost romantic involvement later.

I showered, went to bed, and could not sleep. I thought about us alone at the dinner table, the embarrassment between us, the struggling for subjects to talk about. Each of us waiting for the other, or was it I who was hoping for what he did not feel? The phone rang, and I thought it was Lloyd.

"Margo…It's Mike…Everything okay?"

His voice was strained and hesitant.

"Yes," I said. "I think it is."

"Sure?"

"I … May I come? Good to check your locked door."

I hardly heard myself say yes. I blurted something out because he said, "How's three minutes?"

"Three minutes? Do you live so close?"

"Right at the moment, very." He chuckled, "I'm in the hotel. I'm spending the night here, down the hall from you." His voice turned soft, serious, "I thought it'd be a good idea to have a sheriff on the premises tonight, considering what happened today."

Three minutes! I sat up in bed. My heart was pounding. I looked at my watch. It was only 6:30—we had had an early dinner, allowing Hank and Sally to sit with us. I wondered if I should unlock the door, but in my nightgown? I hadn't brought a robe, only a warm-up suit, and not so good-looking at that. I could meet him outside the door—in what apparel?

I wanted to comb my hair, put on lipstick—and lights? Should I turn the lights on? If I didn't, he'd think that…

There was a knock on the door; I opened it, and without words, Sheriff Montana picked me up, carried me to my Victorian bed.

We passed through cycles as strangers diffident and caring, to where I remember little, except an exquisiteness in clouds of velvet, riding waves of the sea among the pines and snow, the pure mountain air that surrounded the Sierra and in that time we owned it, outside our two worlds left to others, and if that time could stand still—who knew?—forever.

The melting snow outside made a light patter, a sound familiar from childhood, and now it was sweet; it would always be so from then on whenever I heard it. He reached for my hand and held it.

"I want to tell you about Laura's mother." He stopped for a moment, and I was afraid he would not be able to continue. He went on, "I never thought I'd be talking about her again. I'd closed the door on it. On anyone I would ever know after her."

"There was no one after her?"

"Oh, Hank and Sally would try to get me to go out. I'd do it just to please them, but it never amounted to anything. I tried. At the beginning, I wasn't ready anyway. I had my child to raise and I was doing construction work, free-lancing for companies. Then I started my own business, got involved in that, and after a while, Hank and Sally gave up on me. In retrospect I was trying hard to keep myself busy. Less time to think, less time to blame myself. Work's a good medicine.

"The grandparents were a big help. In general terms, they add a good balance to the family. One thing about living in a small town, you either get out or generations stay. Mine were here. Hank and Sally were never able to have children, and when I lost my parents, they were there for me. They also as grandparents for Laura."

"Has she ever come back?"

"Once. Laura was twelve. Old enough to be angry but at that age needing a mother. Jill didn't know how to handle it. She knew Laura was judging her, and she didn't know how to be a mother, to meet a teenager's needs. A few days later, she left us again."

A silvery light from the snow bathed the room, touching objects, throwing shadows; shamelessly we had made love in that magic light, touching, discovering each other. But now there was pain and guilt in his voice as he talked about his wife, reached back into the years.

"We had married young—too young—both of us were nineteen. She was pregnant. Had she not been, I doubt we would have married. Physically she was a frail girl, and maybe that made her more prone…to anything. The pregnancy was hard, and she was depressed for a while after Laura was born. But she seemed to snap out of it, though she complained of being bored. We had her parents for support, in the sense of helping with Laura, as well as Hank and Sally and whatever else, so we all encouraged her to get a job. In hindsight it was probably wrong, but she had no real responsibility at home, and I was often working at my new business. She liked the idea of a job and found one working in one of the hotels in Tahoe. For a time, it was okay until she got mixed up with the wrong crowd—a lot of people who had come from out of town to work so they could ski. Skiing and drugs, that's what they were into. Or at least the ones she had made friends with. Jill was not a skier though. Maybe it would have been better if she had been. I tried to get her interested in it, but she wasn't one who liked the outdoors, she was one who was born in this part of the country but was never really a part of it. She only inherited it. That's where we were different. The result for her was it became one thing: drugs. For a while, I was too busy to notice. A drug problem in a family is not necessarily recognized right away. Or, let's say, it can keep a low profile. The drug user can be clever in hiding it, and family members are in denial. No guilt. Nope, we do not want guilt, so if we don't look too hard, it'll go away.

"Jill's cover was being too tired from work. She blamed her passivity, her listlessness, whatever else on work. I tried to get her to quit, but she said she didn't have that much to do at home and was afraid she'd get depressed again. One day she got careless, left some around the house. I had to face up to it."

He paused, then went on.

"She wouldn't go into treatment. She said she'd stop. For a while, I think she did. But it didn't last long. There was still no way I could get her to leave her job, and I honestly don't think it would have solved anything anyway. By that time, she was hooked. I didn't know what to do. Any direction seemed a dead end. She got thinner, spent longer days in Tahoe, working often on weekends, and I'd go after her. It all became a routine, working late on weekends, my going to pick her up.

"When Laura was four, one day during the week, Jill was not at the hotel in Tahoe, where I picked her up. Police traced her to a motel outside Sacramento with someone she'd picked up in the hotel. They were out of it. Spaced from here to kingdom come. They found it on him. Arrested him and put her in my custody. My wife and mother of my child in my custody. That is how I got my sheriff's badge out of it. To have more control. I don't know how it came to that, honest to God I don't. Somewhere in life she—we—had taken the wrong road and that road was leading straight to Hell. There's no way to explain to people who have never experienced drugs in the family what it's like. It's pain all the time—for everybody. It's being totally helpless." He stopped. "Ah, this is hard."

"Mike, you don't have to. Let it be."

"No. It's just facing it again. Talking about it after such a long time," he raised my hand to his lips. "When you have someone in the family on drugs," he continued, "you either find help for them or put a twenty-four-hour watch on them to make sure they stay clean. Jill refused professional help, so that was that, and I had to work. The third option was hope for the best. That led to her going steadily downhill. The next time she disappeared from home, and we couldn't find her. I didn't know if she was dead or alive until she called days later. Wouldn't say where she was and that was the scenario from then on." He laughed bitterly, "The only thing she seemed to consciously to hang onto was our telephone number. I had two choices: put my energy into some kind of a balanced life for Laura or go off in all directions always searching for Jill. It was my daughter or her mother. But I had reached the point where I didn't want Jill around Laura, if or when she turned up, so the choice was easy. I'm not proud of that. Maybe if I kept pressing it, I would have finally been able to bring her home, but life is made up of a lot of decisions.

"She showed up on her own when Laura was twelve. If there had been a way to stop the pain of that visit…But she took care of that herself by leaving as suddenly as she came. I haven't heard from her since. It's been six years." He sighed, "I guess I should've taken her out of here. Left Truckee, gone to a place entirely new to us. Having grandparents—two sets of them— left her with a lot of time on her hands. If we'd been off on our own some- where, without family, she would've been busy with responsibilities. Not ended up in Tahoe because she needed something to do. I blame myself in that respect. I'm part of this country…to think of leaving…" he laughed, "Indian roots. Out of all of this, I am grateful to the young woman Laura has become. She grew up surrounded by love, the result is she is strong. I don't fear for her. "

He kissed me tenderly. I wanted to say something, find the right words. My answer was only to hold him close, offer myself to him on our field of love in the ash-colored light.

I woke with a start. The room was slipping into the blue-grey light of dawn. I turned and saw Mike pulling his sweater over his head.

"You're leaving," I whispered.

He settled his sweater and came over and sat on the bed. "I was hoping you wouldn't wake up."

I put my arm around him and pulled him down.

"Oh, no," he laughed, "then I'll never get out of here." Seriously he brushed my hair back against the pillow, "Do you know you're very pretty? You make me think of honey…honeysuckles."

"I do? No one has ever described me in such an original way."

"Always a first time. Summer they grow well here," he said, smiling. "You're skin is as fair as…I don't know. It'll come to me later…"

"Which got burned today," I laughed.

"Would've been worse without my cream."

"When was that? A hundred days ago. Two hundred days ago that Lloyd and I left Santa Cruz? And now you're going." I wanted to hold him, keep him with me, for in this room I felt protected from a vague uneasiness, an unreasonable fear more for him than for Lloyd and myself.

"Mike, stay," I said. I sat up and put my arms around him, held him tight.

He laughed, "Let the world go to hell." He set me back against the pillows, fixed the covers firmly around my neck. "You want to go over everything before I leave?"

"If it will keep you here."

"Go over it again."

Obediently I did. "What if the wrong person takes the purse? It'll be offered in plain sight."

"That won't happen. No one other than the person directly interested would do that. People playing the slots are too engrossed in what they are doing. If they're not watching for a win, they're listening for it, and whoever is wandering around is usually studying a machine, wondering which one is not going to cheat."

"You talk like someone who knows," I teased.

"Haven't lived all my life here not to."

He stood up and looked down at me humorously, reached into his back pocket, "I've got a present for you. Some vouchers, worth $15 for the slots. Someone gave them to me, and I had forgotten about them. Don't move," he said, "don't talk." He bent down and kissed me, long and passionately. "If you knew how many times I thought of calling you last night. Another kind of gambling. Go back to sleep," he whispered.

I closed my eyes. I didn't want to watch him leave. I listened to his footsteps, heard the door shut softly. The only reason I was grateful he was leaving at dawn was his avoiding being seen by Lloyd, up early getting the newspaper. I don't know how I would have reacted had that happened. I preferred not to think about it.

Alone in bed, I was drowsily aware of morning filling the room and memories, our night together so careful at first. How passion, with its sudden newness, can still be called upon after so many years. I went over what he had told me about Jill, picturing him with this wife who did not have the strength, who was too fragile, to stay with him. It was only hours ago that I stood watching him ski down a hill with the joy and grace of one who has mountains in his blood. I remembered, too, the isolation I felt as I watched him. Maybe envy, he a part of something and I never had been. Perhaps that had been the way with Jill. She was young, not able to deal with being left out.

I thought of his mother and father killed in an avalanche, of those with hope, those who had worked their way through a mountain, the Mormons who created the city I had lived in, that Lloyd and I were now returning to, and of courage, always fear never allowed to dominate. I thought of journeys in life and the unexpected, mine that brought me to Truckee. With all my heart, I thought of a young child in need of a mother who returned, then disappeared. The age of my students, whose minds were open and accepting yet vulnerable.

I watched the room lighten, the brightness become stronger, to slowly consume the early blue light and then I fell asleep.

11.

I DON'T KNOW HOW LONG LLOYD HAD BEEN KNOCKING AT MY DOOR; certainly long enough for the time it took to pull me from my almost drugged, exhausted sleep. I confused the sounds at first with the patter of the melting snow that grew louder and louder and then I woke with a start thinking of gunshots. As happened the knocking was not that loud, Lloyd torn between wanting to wake me but without commotion.

"Margo?"

I moved heavily toward the door, half dizzy from sleep. Opening it slightly, I said, "What time is it?"

"Almost a quarter to nine."

I caught a glimpse of him already dressed, always smart in his sports jacket with a handkerchief in the pocket. I knew he had shined his shoes, he had that look about him.

"I'll meet you downstairs in twenty minutes," I said.

I walked to the window and looked outside. The sky was a solid, fathomless blue, the trees in the process of shedding snow so sharp and defined, they seemed to have been cut out and set on paper. I could see the majestic, snow-covered mountains looming in the distance, ridged and coned, commanding, hard white against the purple-blue sky. So clear in the pure air, I could almost count the ridges around them. I thought where we would be today, and had plans held their course, Lloyd would now be sitting in a chair in The Hotel Utah and I...I realized I had never had a plan about what I'd do once we arrived there. The plan had only been to get away, at some point having convinced Lloyd it was time to move.

I took a shower, reluctant to wash away any part of last night. I dressed and combed my hair, and in the mirror, smiled at the thought of honeysuckles. The sunburn was fading, but I knew it would not leave me tan—at the most a very pale yellow that never pleased me when I was young, given that I was the only one among my friends who could not acquire a deep, caramel color. Nina used to tease me about it, who had a darker complexion. Now I was a *honeysuckle*. I smiled over this title because in its simplicity the thought was poetic. As youths we were not poetic. I pinned my hair behind my ears, the style I had fashioned these days as a coming-out-party for myself. The blond ends were lighter than the rest, and I pulled strands of them out to frame my face. I stopped for thirty seconds and stared at myself without make-up. He had said I was *pretty*. I was well-acquainted with this face. Now with time, the word *pretty* had acquired an obsoleteness about it. Not a sad obsoleteness, it was just a normal evolvement. When did Dev stop calling me *pretty*? (Because of course he had at one time.) Was there a line that marked when he stopped? A line when I had not expected it anymore? Cared? It all went in block-form with a period in the past. And now another man had called me *pretty*. There was an obligation attached to this opinion. I brought along skin lotion for my face and now carefully applied it, working it in, to protect my fair skin. The fatigue I had felt upon waking had disappeared and was not even reflected in my eyes. In my own home after a whole night's sleep, I could look tired. In this mirror, my eyes looked bright. Had I so desperately needed this night of passion, had I become deprived? And now what was in store? We had made no promises last night. It was only discovery, working through years, a journey for Mike that had been through wastelands, making up for them in a few hours. Today I knew not what he felt. As for myself—well, yes, stronger than I ever felt for Dev.

I slipped on my new jacket, picked up what had become my very important purse, and forced some courage into my thoughts, for not only did I have to deal with futures, there was an extra thrown in and very imminent: The casino.

"I was just going up to get you," Lloyd said as I came out of the elevator. He looked at me slightly pleased. "Why, you look fresh today. Must have been our getting to bed so early last night."

"Do I?" I said taken aback, trying not to laugh. "Thank you. You look pretty nifty yourself."

"Sure I do. We're going out on the town."

Sally brought us coffee and sweet rolls, showing she had quickly learned from Lloyd his desired fare for breakfast. I didn't have much of an appetite and thought it best to conserve the little I had for lunch, to eat with enthusiasm in front of a murderer spying on us because he had not yet tried to nab my purse.

"Maybe you don't remember, but your mother won the jackpot at the slot machine once."

We had both been trying to keep a conversation afloat on the way to the casino. The road was slow-going, filled with cars on their way to Tahoe.

"Oh? When?"

"In Reno. After we were married. She must've won about $35. Not bad in those days. Enough to pay for our wedding dinner for the four of us."

"I forgot all about that," I said. "Nina and I were in the hotel room, Mother came in with her purse full of coins..."

"For dessert we had Baked Alaska, remember that?"

I told him I did, though it was not true. What I did remember was that Nina had been glued to the radio listening to Inner Sanctum in our hotel room, a program that we never missed, conveniently on that evening as kids weren't allowed to hang around gambling machines.

We found ourselves talking about their getting married, our taking what was then called *The Milk Train* to Reno from Salt Lake. Checking into the hotel, then going to the Justice of the Peace. He remembered small things, things that had completely escaped me. But then it was *their* day. I camouflaged my forgetfulness with other questions, feeding his memory, both of us clinging to the past, a way of finding diversion in the face of the casino plan. Silently I recalled reading once an article on the attempted assassination of a president of the United States. It concluded if someone wanted to kill the president, he would find a way. So where did that put us? More accessible targets, I guessed, not having the protection of the presidents. Then I had to remind myself that first he wanted my purse (The piece on the roller coaster had been placed in a safety vault in the hotel. In its place, a torn page from the hotel brochure describing Truckee—in case he grabbed my purse and had time to pull out what he thought he was looking for).

Lloyd kept glancing in the rear-view mirror, and the only mention of our mission in going to the casino was when I asked him if he noticed anyone following us.

"Hell, who knows?" he said. Feigning indifference. "We're all locked up in line here, which makes it easy for anyone to follow us. I'm keeping my eyes on the road, and that's it."

But I knew if he could have guided the car looking in the rear-view mirror, he would have done it. He had insisted on driving, something I understood due to male ego and control in a testy situation. I hadn't wanted to enter into a discussion with him, it being useless. I was thankful it was not far. Mike's car—Hank's—we could not see, but we had the directions along with a couple of road signs with arrows indicating CASINO.

It was not long before we pulled into the wide parking area of the casino. As promised there was a space for the car right in front of the entrance. The parking lot was full, and I wondered how a space was kept for us. I did not linger on that thought more than it figured that it was obvious to whoever wanted my purse saw clearly our parked car. Proof we were there. We pulled into it. Both of us got out. Lloyd locked the car and promptly walked away with the key still in the lock.

"Margo, you go on, I'll go back and get them," he said while I reminded myself we were not safely in a grocery store parking lot. I accompanied him to retrieve the keys. People were walking to and from the casino, and I wondered where Mike was. Clearly he was keeping a distance. I was also impressed that gamblers started early. It then occurred to me undercover police—perhaps. An assurance Mike gave us. We are in their hands.

My new boots remained dry thanks to the cleared parking area; a thick rug trimmed in gold lay before the casino entrance.

The place was crowded. The bright white lights from chandeliers bounced off the colored neon ones that lit up the ubiquitous slots and beer ads and the gambling tables. The colors fluttered over the crowd in red, greens, and yellows, over men wearing ranger hats and plaid shirts, those in ski clothes, and women in tight jeans with high-heeled boots who were indifferently working the handles of the slot machines. My feet sank into the plush rug that absorbed the sharp noise of the tumbling, shuffling ring of money, reducing it to a continuous low-keyed hum, yet strong enough to block out human voices.

"We have to get some coins with the vouchers Mike gave me," I said as we stood in the center of it all, looking around in a befuddled way.

"What a waste of time," he said to me as we stood there. "People throwing their money away like that…"

"Look chipper," I added quietly, "remember, we're here for a good time."

Obediently his voice rose, too high, "Let's do the dimes!"

"Too much zeal is not recommend either," I whispered as we walked through the crowd searching for the counter to change the vouchers, my purse over my shoulder and firmly held in front of me, not wanting to risk it being taken before set in its proper place on the stool next to where I would be gambling.

"So we'll do the dimes then?" I said to Lloyd.

"Fine with me."

Having changed the vouchers for rolls of dimes, we found the two machines, numbers on them waiting for us, on an aisle as planned. I was relieved. He and I divided our rolls between us.

In the few times I have played slot machines, I have never won much to speak of, but this time, third try, I was granted a slew of coins. I let the coins sit there, like gamblers did, proof of indifference because I knew—felt it—I was being watched. The eerie feeling had crept from the back of my neck to my fingers, made them tingle, placed me in an atmosphere of tension, isolating me from everyone else, and that person was waiting also—we had become one as we clung to time. My purse was placed in such a way that I could see it out of the corner of my eye while I played, yet still obviously easy for someone to walk by and slip it away. I knew when that happened, Lloyd and I would be set free, it would be over, the police would nab him.

I heard money fall from Lloyd's machine and looked over at him. He was engrossed in playing, sincere pleasure on his face, now putting the money back in as fast as anything dropped in the metal bowl.

When I turned back, it was in time to catch Marshall approaching.

"Marshall," I exclaimed laughing, relieved seeing a familiar face, even if it was Marshall's. "What are you doing in Truckee? Is Dorrie here?"

"This *is* a coincidence," he pulled up beside me. "How's it going, Lloyd?" He reached over and shook Lloyd's hand, who had stopped playing and had been looking at him in surprise.

"Well, I'll be damned. Never expected to see you here. Where's Dorrie?"

"She's back home. I'm just passing through. You both have a good trip?"

"Good enough," I said, hoping in my heart of hearts that Lloyd would not bring up the subject of the murder. But I saw something in his eyes that told me he wouldn't. I had not forgotten the importance of my purse and now wondered what we were going to do. At any rate, I was still glad to see even Marshall.

He asked us if we had had lunch.

"Not yet," I said.

"How about us doing it then," he said.

We helped Lloyd gather up his coins, I got mine, took my purse, and we strolled off to the restaurant.

The restaurant wasn't crowded, and we easily found a booth. The three of us slipped into it, Lloyd first, then Marshall, myself across from them. The waitress came over and set the table: glasses of ice water, knives, forks, menus.

Lloyd said as he opened a menu, "I like your tweed coat, Marshall. You needed something like that with the snow," and he caught my eye as Marshall picked up his menu.

Cold fear took hold of me, solid as steel. Like a flash, it all was there, vivid in a matter of not even seconds. Terror gave precision to it. Marshall! Our dinner party, talk of our trip, Minnie's money, the treasure hunt, the information about the roller coaster in my purse. He had all he wanted to know, even the hotel, for we had talked about that also. The fitting together of it, the shock, the knowledge in those moments took my breath away.

Lloyd knew, and with a look, had passed this on to me—the tweed coat, the back of it on the person he had seen walking away on our floor—after he had searched my room.

I don't know how I found the words to suit the indifferent tone I hoped to take, except when under pressure, let's say life-threatening, one does and obviously I had succeeded because Marshall showed no sign of suspicion.

"Say," he said pleasantly, "do you still have the information on the roller coaster? I wouldn't mind reading it now that we are here sitting down. It's a rare piece of history."

I picked up my bag, telling him I wasn't sure if I had left it in the hotel. My hands were shaking. Lloyd noticed and launched into one of his stories— a new one and had to do with a Chicago restaurant and how a gangster had broken into it while he—Lloyd—was there and shot someone...I knew he was making it up, it wouldn't have taken—certainly Lloyd—all these years to have gotten around to a story like that.

What happened was fast. Mike, who slipped into our booth next to me, across from Marshall and saying he'd like to talk to him, Marshall, in what were seconds, pulling a gun and shooting Mike, then bolting, police who blocked his way, in the distance a shot fired, my kneeling beside Mike who had fallen to the floor, blood seeping from him, blood that would not stop, my hand hovering over him—seeking the right place to light as if touching that secret spot would stop the bleeding while wanting to cry out, to call upon my mother, maybe I did as I cradled his head, hearing my voice telling him to stay with us, telling him not to leave us until someone drew me away.

I did not know where Lloyd was. I found him later in his car, where I was led. A policeman drove us back to the hotel, we obviously not in a complete stable state to do it ourselves.

I stared numbly from the car window, the cold white of the land stretching, stretching, where it pulled up to the edge of the mountains, those mountains that thrust themselves into the dense, purple sky—mountains that I now hated for I felt this had been planned by them, by *her*, the Sierra, who gave and took at whim. Who felt threatened and did not want to release Mike. Who, if she could not have him, no one could. I shut my eyes. *You cannot take at will. You do not have power over others' lives. You are not God! YOU ARE NOT GOD!* I tried to calm myself. Do not think. Rest the mind in space, for there is nothing you can do to change things. Nothing. Nothing. Yet I could not push away the sight of Mike crumpled on the floor, the blood seeping, his face so pale as they lifted him onto the stretcher, outside the shrill pumping sound from the waiting ambulance, people being held back, and the stretcher hurrying through, a path opened for it, disappearing, someone gripping my arm...I remember the siren full-blast fading into the distance...

I had asked to be taken to the hospital, we having left Lloyd at the hotel to eventually answer questions by the police. Through the car window, I raised my hand to him as we drove away, he returned the gesture only with a look of agony in his eyes.

The policeman, after driving me to the hospital, had been very kind. He accompanied me through the hospital and up to the small waiting room for those who had someone in intensive care. If it hadn't been for him, I doubt that I would have been able to convince anyone I had a right—which I didn't, not being a member of the family, nor holding any other similar role; I discovered later he was also the one who had gently pulled me away after Mike was shot. We rode the elevator in silence, the heavy hospital odor, an invisible mist everywhere, barely parting our path, and it made my stomach turn. As a hospital for healing, I feared them, for they symbolized more death to me than life and hope. What little I had known of them, the illness part, had been due to my father whose life had ended there, as also a good friend's. The policeman left me at the entrance to the waiting room. It was only after he left that it occurred to me I did not thank him.

Laura, Mike's daughter, was in the room, though I doubt she was aware of my entering. She was sitting stiff and straight in a chair, hands tightly clasped in her lap, her head resting back against the wall. Her eyes were closed. Yes, how much she looked like her father, only now her face ghostly, its whiteness an alarming contrast to her black hair. Was she thinking of her mother, and does need for a mother ever pass, even for Laura, hers she barely knew? For myself, an older woman, I had not yet shed the need of mine after I had left my marriage. I wanted to say something to her, go over and touch her, I wanted to show her that if nothing else, she was not alone. But I felt an intruder in the room, this place where waiting was a family affair. How could she know my excuse for intrusion was that sometimes on this earth, one finds love unexpectedly, yet so sure about it as I? That my loss if Mike died would be my own kind of devastation. If only I could tell her these things, if she would believe it and understand.

~~~

I sat down quietly in a too deep, too comfortable leather chair. The luxury of it did not fit this room. Laura had chosen the correct one: to allow her to sit tall and straight, in dignity to wait for bad news or good ones. *Oh, God, I thought, if there is a God, and if there is, I have no right to ask when I have never praised in happy times, but if there is, yet what point to finish?* The God knows what I feel, what both of us feel sitting in this room.

The door to the room was partly open. I could hear the soft shuffling of nurses' shoes, louder their good-humored voices used to making the best of situations, joking and talking about past snowstorms or who was to take a break for coffee. The sun, strong as yesterday, sent its bright rays through the Venetian blind on the one window, made a ladder pattern on the floor, on a table, and the few magazines scattered on it. On the wall above the table was a framed photograph of a skier ripping through deep snow, flurries in his wake like white sawdust. I went over and picked up a magazine, brought it back to my chair, and set it on my lap. *Money Magazine.* On the cover was mentioned its articles, one on retiring and investing, another on choosing a stock broker. I didn't open it. It just felt good to rest my hands on it; it was cool, and the pages were slick. Moments of slickness a comfort. The subjects distant. Time had come to a halt. We were wedged in it. Yet why was so much of it passing? Why were the nurses still laughing and joking? I tried sorting through my thoughts to find something strong to distract me.

You must know—our mother told us, the three of us alone without husband and father—*the courage we find now will be on file, to pull out other times in life when we must look for it. It will remind us that if we had found it once, it could be found again.* To me then, it seemed no solution for the pain from loss—of course no solution to making the mean kids nice to me, the *new one*, in school. But we made it. That history must be somewhere in the file.

There was now a quiet from the nurses. So quiet that outside the closed window, I could hear the birds chirping. I tried to sort out what happened at the casino. Marshall. It was impossible to believe. It was asking the maximum of credibility. I went back over the times I had been with him. There was nothing seducing about him, nothing smooth about him: he was not a likeable guy. In that sense, there was no deception. But a murderer? He was macho and self-centered and treated Dorrie with little respect, and even if we weren't quite sure what he did for a living and made a home in a trailer, was this indicative of a deadly side? He was not an open person about himself, except for opinions on subjects. What did this signify? A portent sign of a murderer's taste? After these facts, everything now seemed to have an ominous meaning. And Dorrie! My God, Dorrie! What is she thinking—doing—having suddenly found out she is married to a murderer? I wondered how she could live with a man and not know, suspect, the terrible things he was capable of. He had killed two people without warning, had shot Mike—without warning— and who knows what he might have done to Lloyd and me if he had somehow obtained the information and didn't need me—us—anymore. This man had been our guest over my mother's table cloth at the dinner table while Dorrie was kind—and vulnerable, surely in denial. As I had been, until I knew I could not live with Dev, another kind of murderer. As Mike, his difficulty in accepting the addiction of his wife. Wrap us up in a package because we were, all of us, in denial.

"Miss Montana?"

The surgeon was standing in the doorway. He had a robin-egg blue surgeon's coat on, a blue cap on his head. He looked first at me since I was opposite the door. He followed my glance to Laura.

Laura jumped and opened her eyes. She fixed them wide with terror on the doctor.

"He'll be fine. He's lost some blood, but you've got a lucky father. And a strong one. The bullet just grazed the liver, and we got the bullet out. He's had a transfusion, and we were able to match his blood without a problem. In about an hour, you can go in to the intensive care unit to see him."

He smiled kindly at Laura, then told her he had to leave to operate on another patient. A nurse would call her when it was time.

Laura rose to her feet to thank him but seemed on the verge of collapse. The doctor and I rushed over to her. We guided her to the couch in the room.

"Are you okay?" he asked. Laura nodded. "He'll be fine," he reassured her. "He'll be in and out of it today but up and around tomorrow." He looked at me. "Are you part of the family?"

"No," I said. "Just a friend. I'll stay here with Laura."

The surgeon nodded and left.

"Yes, he's strong," said Laura. Her voice quavered, "He's always been strong."

She began to cry.

I drew her to me, held her in my arms as her mother would have, as Jill would have done.

After a few moments, she drew away. She fumbled in her purse for a handkerchief, found it, and dabbed her eyes. "Margo—it's Margo, isn't it? Do you know what happened?"

Her eyes were pained, steady on me, a deep blue, the one sure feature about her that could be her mother's.

I sighed. "I don't even know where to begin," I answered wearily. "The whole situation is still hard for me to believe. To sum it up as far as Sheriff Montana is concerned, my step-father and I stopped in Truckee on the way to Salt Lake, and I dumped a problem in his lap. From then on, he became my—our bodyguard."

I began from our leaving Santa Cruz, trying to relate from being followed, backtracking to the older couple we had visited, the roller coaster information, from there to Mike being shot, and then Marshall. It filled easily the time waiting for the nurse to give Laura permission to see her father

Laura's face was still very pale. She said softly, "All they told me when I got to the hospital was they had taken him straight to surgery. No one could tell me anything else. I didn't know if Daddy was dying. I thought he could be. That maybe he had." Her eyes brimmed with tears, she took a deep breath. "My mother…Daddy is all I have."

"I know," I whispered.

"You know?"

"We had time to talk. Many things can be said in two days of almost constant company."

"What did you do? Where did you go?"

"Well, first of all, I got the ski clothes from *you*," and I smiled at her, "we went to lunch and then we went skiing."

"That's my father," she laughed, color returning to her pale face, "always finding a good excuse to go up the mountain."

"He loves the mountains, doesn't he?"

"He grew up here. He'd never leave."

"So did you."

"But I could leave. I love Truckee, the Sierra, but I know I could leave."

"Have you ever thought of it?"

"Sometimes," she said wistfully. "I don't think leaving my father being alone is holding me back. He's very independent. He'd be alright. It's fear—probably that. It's wanting to strike out on my own but at the same time afraid to do it. Not that I haven't taken some steps. I'm studying toward a degree here in social work—I've always been interested in working with minorities, the poor, but meanwhile I got into selling clothes. I don't know…I guess you go just where life leads you."

She paused, thoughtful for a moment.

"Maybe," she went on, "one day it'll take me somewhere else…to find my mother. I believe that's always been in the back of my mind. Ever since I was old enough to understand why she left, and it really wasn't her fault. When I was younger, sometimes I would dream about finding her," she laughed, "there'd be a detective with me, we'd go to a hospital, she'd be in a room tired and sick, or we'd find her on a street corner as a bag lady—that of course was the worst dream. One time we walked into a restaurant and there she was working, cured. She was ashamed to come home. But hers is a world…I wouldn't know where to start. And way down there in my subconscious is probably why I got interested in social work." She murmured almost to herself, "Someday, through that work, I'd come upon her, I'd find her that way and take care of her…"

Jill, I thought. A phantom to me and yet…I saw the color of her eyes in her daughter, I had made love with the man who had done the same with her, I loved him, as she had at one time before her mind became fogged with drugs, and I was here now listening to the dreams of her daughter.

"But," she took up, "…I'm afraid it would be difficult for my father, her leaving us was so hard on him…alone…with a small child to raise. Now for him, it's in the past. It wouldn't be right to bring back so many painful memories."

"Maybe one day you could do it on your own. Quietly—a closure. For her, too. As a mother, I would want to see you. Oh, so much." The more I listened to Laura, watched her, I was taken by the air of fragility about her, a quality I imagined in her mother, yet strength that Jill obviously lacked. My role, an interloper, touched by two lives. Both settled into who they are. Mountains cultivated aloneness; real love reflected in a daughter.

Time put in as a single parent, result a lovely young woman one who nurtured a plan for the future.

Laura was looking at me thoughtfully, "But if she's dead...I've never had a dream that she was. It's curious that I never dreamed she was..." Her voice trailed off. "But what about you?" she said brightly. "Do you have a family? I would imagine that you have."

"Oh? Why?"

"You seem so understanding."

"I left my marriage two years ago. We did not have children and a blessing."

"I'm sorry. I'm truly sorry."

"It's alright, Laura. I came to terms with it while still married."

"We all have our troubles, don't we?" she said. "It strengthens one, they say. Though I think I'd rather get mine from a sugar overdose."

Both of us laughed over this.

"Laura," I said, "we're—my step-father and I—we're probably leaving to-morrow to continue on to Salt Lake City as we had planned. Do you suppose it would be possible...would you mind...if I went in to see your father? That is if they would give the okay? I...it's just that I am so grateful..." but I stopped there. I didn't know what else to say to ask for this. I was a stranger to her, without rights.

She smiled at me, "I think it's very kind of you to want to do that. Of course you can."

"I'll wait here through the day," I said. "Then if there's a good moment... I appreciate it, I really do."

Shortly after our agreement, a nurse arrived to tell Laura she could be with her father. He was doing well, and with this second piece of positive news, I saw the tenseness leave her body. Given permission to go to him, she left so quickly, she dropped her purse, the nurse sweeping it up and running after her. I telephoned the hotel and left a message about Mike. I talked to Hank, whose voice was tight and apprehensive when I called, and I could envision the relief in his face when I told him Mike would pull through and explained what the surgeon had told us. Lloyd was talking with the police, he said.

I waited in the room watching the light change to late afternoon, the sun through the blinds touching objects, the light growing heavier with the passing of the day. I fingered the magazines, thumbed through an article on Montana ranches. It seemed an endless length of time after the shooting this morning. It was impossible to picture Mike fighting to regain his strong life—though now Laura had come in the waiting room with the news he was out of intensive care and in his own room not far away. I could only envision the healthy person who had captivated me when I had gone to his office with the story of being followed. Nor was I able to erase the image of the fallen one as they carried him away.

"Margo."

I turned. Lloyd was standing in the doorway.

"How's Mike?"

"They've taken him out of intensive care. He'll be fine. The bullet nicked the liver, and he lost some blood. They gave him a transfusion. I'm hoping to see him for a few minutes."

"Thank the Lord."

"Didn't you get my message? I talked with Hank."

"No. The police drove me here before I had a chance to talk to him."

Compared to his dapperness hours ago, he looked disheveled—for Lloyd—his handkerchief crooked in his breast pocket and his bow tie tipped.

"There's some coffee in the hall. Do you want me to bring you a cup?" I asked.

"That'll be just fine." He sat down in a chair.

I realized as I got the coffee, I hadn't had anything to eat since breakfast, meager at that with little inclination to eat then, now afraid to leave and miss Laura, who could have come for me anytime to see Mike.

"Tell me," said Lloyd as I returned with his coffee, "have you had anything to eat?"

"Not since this morning."

"Go get something. There's a cafeteria downstairs. I'll stay here."

"I think I won't. Thanks. I'd like to see Mike. His daughter, Laura, was going to bring me to him any time."

"What about tomorrow? You can see him tomorrow." I caught a testiness in his voice.

"I thought I'd talk to you, Lloyd, about leaving. Go on to Salt Lake. He'll have so many visitors tomorrow, we'd be in the way."

Lloyd picked right up on the idea. "That was in my mind, too. You beat me to it. We've brought trouble on Mike and now his daughter. If it weren't for us stopping, here none of it would have happened. I guess it goes without talking that it could have been worse for us someplace else."

"What did the police say? Hank said you were talking with them."

"They wanted to know about our visit to the apartment, how we got the info on the roller coaster. Shucks, I must've told them the same thing twenty times. This whole thing...Marshall...I guess the most important story of my life was waiting for me now, towards the end of it. Jesus."

"Where is he? Was he shot? I heard a shot after he ran off from shooting Mike."

"Lucky for him—or unlucky for us because he should've been killed. He was shot in the shoulder. He's here in the hospital. Before coming here, I went to see him."

"My God, Lloyd! You went to see Marshall? Well, that takes—I don't know what. The idea sickens me. Just picturing him in my mind sickens me. I'd like to keep only the image of him as he was, just an obnoxious person."

"As we know, he was more than that, and I wanted to confront him with it. For Dorrie's sake—married to a good woman like her. The whole thing makes me more than sick. Anyway they also wanted me to confirm his identity, which I was happy and sorry to do. Better if it had been the nephew. We got a long way off course from that, didn't we? Goes to show one can't judge by appearances. But let's admit, the nephew was a perfect fit at the time. I also wanted to be the first to tell him what he had gone to all this trouble for was only $2,000. Breaking that news to him suited me just fine."

"What...what did he do when he saw you?"

"Not a damn thing. Just looked at me. He was in bed with his shoulder in a cast. Too good of a place for him. The son of a bitch—excuse my French. Then the policeman, who was in the room, asked me to sign a paper verifying it was Marshall who was looking at me. And of course, verifying he was the one who shot Mike. Which I did. Finally Marshall said, 'The whole thing sucks, doesn't it, Lloyd?' I said you're damn right it does. What the hell did you do it for, Marshall? 'Money,' he said. But you killed them, I said. 'It wasn't in my mind to do that,' he answered. 'I don't know what was in my mind. No plan. After you and Margo talked about your visit there, I thought I'd wander over. See if they'd found the will—maybe money stashed somewhere. I told them I heard the apartment was for rent. They let me in. They were pretty excited. They'd just found this note. They showed it to me. It'd been taped under the dining room table. It was written by the woman who died. It said she had left some money and she'd left a code where to find it on something written, history about the roller coaster. It was in a kitchen drawer, the note said. She called it a treasure hunt and felt the money was safe that way. Pretty odd. The couple remembered it was what they had given Margo. They knew the answer was on that. I knew Margo had it because she said so at dinner, at your place. Was in her purse.'"

Lloyd said, "After that he just out and out shot them. He told me he figured they were old, so it didn't matter much. It was clean. They hadn't suffered. I said that was damn thoughtful of him. He needed the money, he said. Can you beat that? And he didn't even have the excuse of being a crazed drug addict. One thing I forgot to ask him was he had a gun with him and did he carry a gun with him all the time? He must have planned it, Margo. Or taken a gun with him just in case. And he would have told me if I asked him. He was so damn open about it all.

"I asked him where the nephew was, and the couple told him—before he killed them that is—that he'd gone back to wherever he lived. He had a problem with drugs, they told him—one thing you and I were right about, if it makes us happy to be right about something. Marshall said he figured the blame would be put on the nephew. He messed up the house to make it look like a robbery, maybe give the idea the nephew was looking for something, who knows what? He knew our plans to take a trip to Salt Lake, you had the information he wanted in your purse, so he followed us. Took care of the car tire to keep us there for his next move. He figured he had it made at lunch when he brought up the subject of the roller coaster. You'd pull it from your purse, he'd find the last clue on it because you knew nothing about it. He'd memorize it. He hadn't counted on Mike. He'd seen you with him in Truckee, and when Mike slipped into the booth, he knew he had to get out and fast. The rest is history."

Lloyd sat back in the chair and looked at me. "I don't know how much Dorrie knew about him, and I'd like to think she was in the dark. I can't imagine her putting up with him otherwise. He has a jail record as seems at one time he was living with a woman, beat her up, and robbed her. I guess it wasn't considered serious enough to keep him behind bars forever. This was years ago. All before Dorrie. To add more wood to the fire, when he got out, he changed his name. Forged papers and got a job teaching at a community college. How and what, I can't imagine. I got all this information from the police by the way. I was amazed at how fast it all came through. Been sitting around all these years. So…that's it. Except for one more thing: Marshall, I said, looking him straight in the eyes, would you have killed us if you had to? 'Good question, Lloyd,' he said. 'Don't know. You're alive. Be glad about it.' "

"What did he say when you told him the hidden money was only $2,000?"

"After that I walked out of the room. I didn't tell him. By then I pitied the guy. I didn't want to see his reaction. I figured I just couldn't kick someone when he's down, or would be after that fact. And may I add just one thought: how you never know people. Let's say applied to Marshall. Makes one wonder." He stopped, "You know what came to mind coming here on the elevator? The one who might inherit his money could be the nephew."

I sighed, "Well, Lloyd, maybe he'll mend his way. Drop the drug habit."

I got up and walked over to the window. I widened two slats of the blinds and looked outside. We were over a parking lot that was half-full. I thought of the blue car. All the time it was Marshall in that car. I parted streams, rivers, and oceans thinking back as I stood at the window, to our dinner that evening, to Dorrie, and always Marshall, his killing the couple, where he had gone after the crime—home to Dorrie, the dinner she cooked, his getting his blue car gassed up to follow us…? I could not get enough of imagining. It overwhelmed me.

"I called Junie," Lloyd said suddenly.

I turned. "Oh, you did?" I saw a light just briefly dance in his eyes.

"She said there've been police all over. It was on the radio about Mike being hurt, and you can be sure about *us*. It's damn good we're going to Salt Lake. Give things time to calm down. Of all people who had to have something to do with a drug addict hippy, it had to be me. Do you want me to get you something to eat and bring it up here?"

"I guess so. I should eat something, shouldn't I?"

"What do you want?"

"Anything. A salad, a hamburger. You decide."

I watched him leave, appreciating not having to make even a minor decision. I opened a magazine for the umpteenth time and must have dozed off for a moment because someone had lightly touched my arm, made me jump.

"Margo? I'm sorry. I didn't mean to startle you." It was Laura. "He's been asleep for quite a while. I think he's on the verge of waking. You've been here such a long time, maybe you'd like to come now in case he does. He probably won't stay awake very long. It was the loss of blood more than anything else that weakened him, and they say the best way to get back his energy is to sleep."

"I'd like to, Laura."

The room was quiet, except for one of the machines hooked up to him. Dusk was falling, graying the room, and I had to adjust my eyes to it after the bright hospital corridor. I stood at the foot of the bed. The machine made a low hum, almost imperceptible. Mike lay wounded, injured, under the covers. How had it come to this? I felt a terrible ache in my heart. I walked over to the side of the bed, opposite Laura. Mike's head was turned away from me. He seemed still asleep.

"Daddy," Laura whispered, leaning down over him, "Daddy?"

"Oh, please, don't wake him, Laura," I said. But he had already stirred. He turned his head and looked at me, stared for a moment, then smiled. "Margo…"

"Hi, Sheriff Montana," I said softly, "just came to say hello."

"No more worries for you and Lloyd now."

"No," I said. "No more worries. How do you feel?"

"Tired…but I'll be fine."

"The powder snow's waiting for you."

"Seems a long time ago since yesterday, doesn't it?" He slipped his hand from the covers, and I took it, held it. It was cold. I forced myself not to bring it to my lips. Lay my cheek against it, to warm it. He smiled at me, and I wanted to tell him that I loved him. Tell him that I would never forget the love he had given me last night. I wanted to smooth his black hair where with each stroke, it would make him stronger, to stretch myself the length of his body, lie against the wounded part of him, heal it with my own against his.

And, oh, I wanted to say, "My love, my only love, how did we miss each other? How was it time put us together only now?"

"Is Lloyd okay?" Mike asked. "He's not so young for this kind of thing."

"He's fine. He's been sitting in the waiting room with me," I smiled, "keeping me company with his stories. Now he's gone downstairs to bring me something to eat."

"Tell him he's a brave guy."

"I will. Yet if it hadn't been for you…"

"Somebody else would have done it in my place," he finished for me. "Who…was he? He wasn't the nephew, was he?"

"No," I replied. "It's not important now. Later Laura can tell you. Just gain your strength back." I could see he was tiring, his hand slackened. I released it and gently placed it back under the covers.

"He's ready to sleep again," Laura whispered.

"Yes, I'll go now."

Laura walked me to the door, then turned and took my hand, "I'll always remember your support today. It…meant so much." She grabbed my arm enthusiastically, "Tell me. What are your plans about the trip, now that you can go without worries?"

"We have a bit of a drive to Salt Lake and we leave tomorrow morning. We're staying at the Hotel Utah, a place where Lloyd lived before he married my mother. I believe it has been re-modeled, and I hope it won't be a shock to him. It's been a while since he's been back. For me, too."

"It does sound adventurous, both of you going off like that."

"At least it began that way," I laughed. "But I'm wondering now if the trip might seem boring."

I tried to sound carefree, to equal Laura's enthusiasm.

I turned to look at Mike before leaving. The room was folded in the dark velvet gray of evening now, a peaceful and serene calmness about it, and I knew he was sleeping in a good way. Laura embraced me, her cheek warm and soft against mine. "Don't disappear from our lives. Let's keep in touch. I'll let you know how Daddy progresses. He's not much into letter writing, but I'll prod him. If he doesn't write, I will."

The waiting room held the odor of hamburger that Lloyd had brought; it was wrapped in foil set next to the magazines. There was also a Coke and fries. I was not hungry. I sat down and stared at it.

"What's the matter? You wanted something else?"

"No, it's fine." I picked up the hamburger, folded back the foil, then set it down.

"Lloyd, I can't eat it. I'm sorry."

"What's wrong? It's Mike?" he asked alarmed.

"No. He'll be alright."

"I'll get you something else to eat."

"No...I just want to cry a minute." I pulled out a Kleenex from my purse and did just that. He waited patiently.

I finally got control of myself.

"Well," he said as I dried my eyes, "a good cry never hurt anybody. What's the problem? Without wanting to be too nosey, is it Sheriff Montana?"

"I suppose you can say that."

"Look, we can stay another day."

"Let's just leave as planned."

"How's he feel about it?"

"I'm afraid he's not in the best position to think of anything else right now," I answered too sarcastically and immediately was sorry.

"I grant you that, but you can still stick around. I can drive back to Santa Cruz. You leave from here to Washington. Salt Lake we can do another time."

"Oh, Lloyd," I looked at him, and he was dead serious. "I wouldn't think of having you do that," I said sorrowfully. "Furthermore I'd never stay here on my own. He has his daughter to watch over him these days, friends, and in a small town, there are usually many. But most of all, I don't know if he'd want me. He was fine before I came; he's a man of the mountains—independent, used to his surroundings. We just met each other too late in our lives."

"If that's the way you feel, I'll stay out of it."

"That's the way I feel."

"He's a helluva nice guy, Margo."

"He asked for you. He was worried."

"About what?"

"Well, you aren't that young anymore."

"Oh, shucks, I'm fine. I hope you told him that."

"I think I did."

"Well, then tomorrow. Let's get the show on the road."

He finished drinking the Coke that he had brought for himself, that was in a cup, and I realized it was the first time I had ever seen him not drink it from a bottle.

Saying goodbye to Hank and Sally was harder than I had anticipated. They had been so kind to us. And I know they enjoyed Lloyd's company. Sally insisted on packing us a lunch, so we wouldn't have to eat at one of the "greasy, fast-food places on the road." Or if we did, we'd only have to buy drinks, she said. I could see how they had easily filled the role of being present for Mike after the loss of his parents. More than friends, substitute parents. They had already made plans on how to care for him once back in his home.

"A man alone is never alone in Truckee," Sally said.

"Unless he wants to be," Hank added, raising his eyebrows at her. I assumed he was referring to skiing.

I stood in front of the hotel waiting for Lloyd to bring the car from around the back where it was parked. I could not go there. Memories too strong of kneeling in the cold, finding the gash in the tire, car keys frozen in my hand, myself paralyzed with fear that I was not proud of. No, front was better.

Outside the morning air was cool and very calm, the sun strong. I turned and looked toward her, she with large patches of snow, like white discarded garments fallen without a pattern, waiting to be absorbed by the warm spring air. She had lent us a late snowfall, and I was grateful. As a friend, I raised my hand in salutation, for I felt she was my friend but without favorites. She was a just mountain. One that held a symbol of life.

Before leaving Truckee, we rode through town. Lloyd said he hadn't had a chance to see it after so many years, and I was looking for a store that sold cassettes, having discovered there was a cassette player in his car. Always taking the car for only short outings in Santa Cruz, I had never bothered to look, and Lloyd hadn't thought to remind me because he never used it, being a radio person. But the store wasn't open, so I put it off until Salt Lake. It was the third day of bright sun, and it left nothing untouched, its magical morning rays springing off of everything: roofs, the snow still on the ground, the bright colors of store fronts, even the cars, their chrome sending splinters of light into the air. Behind the town the tall pines reared healthy dark green against the brilliant blue sky.

"A damn nice town," Lloyd said. "Wouldn't mind living here myself, if I had a reason to."

We passed Laura's boutique. There were pretty, colorful dresses still in the window, the reminder that this would be the last snowstorm. I hadn't told Lloyd about the store, nor anything yet about Laura, except that she was Mike's daughter. There'd hardly been time. For the past days, we'd been careening down a slope of what seemed miles an hour. Here, at the end, there were days in front of us to sort things out. Mainly why I had thought of the trip in the first place, and until this moment, it had completely left my mind: to find the situation to convince Lloyd it was time to move. The idea now seemed rusty and useless. I had lost the will and decided I would leave it to Nina on her trip. For there was Junie, who had arrived in the picture.

It was not too late in the morning that we again found ourselves on the road continuing our trip to Salt Lake. On my turn driving, I periodically checked the rear-view mirror—I had not quite lost the habit for blue cars. Remnants of snow hugged in clumps on the mountain-side bordering the highway, soot-gray, and sending a steady stream of water into the recesses along the side of the road—the white beauty of snow lost to problems of aging. At a certain point, we could see the Truckee River, transparent and cold-looking, the wet rocks it brushed glistening in the sun. Then we reached flat land: the desert—where the bee-line strip of asphalt is famous in Nevada and speed can creep up on you, the gray ribbon hypnotically persistent, forever running ahead. Now there were four lanes, but I remembered trips with our father when there were only two, and to pass a car meant patience so as not to ram into one coming from the other direction. Impatience or honking never seemed to prevail. That was the way it was then. We did not live in the future.

As we drove through Nevada, then Utah, Lloyd called off the cities, all of them places where he had been on business, or in Reno—*Reno: 20 Miles*—but we did not talk about stopping. It belonged to *his* memory, marrying our mother there, and frankly, my not a very observant teenager at the time; I remembered little about the chapel, and perhaps Lloyd knew this, too. His memories were locked in that special past and so be it.

Sparks—"Dave Hartman managed the theater there," Lloyd commented when we passed the exit. "Nice man, but he drank a lot." *Lovelock*—"That's where I spent the hottest day of my life one summer." *Winnemucca*—"Had a lobster once for dinner there, right in the middle of the desert, and no different from San Francisco." *Elko*—"Good beef, if you want a steak for dinner." He had a story about them all. When we crossed into Utah: *Wendover*—"First theater out of Salt Lake that played *Gone with the Wind*." *Knolls*...

Soon we began skirting the Great Salt Lake, famous for its high density of salt—second only to The Dead Sea—with just one living creature, a thread-sized shrimp. I hated the lake. Most young people did. It was tantalizingly-silky-smooth, always blue, the water temperature just right and impossible to swim in, unless one didn't mind keeping the mouth tightly shut so not to choke on the salt. The lake was enclosed by a perfect beach for sunning, not at all popular because the salt left a white covering on the body that kept one from acquiring a tan. I went once during my teenage years and never returned. Now as it came into view, I had thoughts about it that were ominous with the Donner tragedy in mind.

On the trip, I had recounted the Donner tale to Lloyd, who knew few details about the tragedy: the miscalculation of the softness of the surface of salt when passing over it with wagon wheels and had slowed the party down. When we reached it, Lloyd wanted to stop and see for himself what it would have been like to have passed over it with heavy wagons. If the surface had been hard, I read, they would have made it before the deadly snow storm.

"I'll tell you one thing," he said, stepping on the whitish surface, "it's the first time in my life I've ever set foot on this territory. And I've driven by it many times." His shoes sunk part way into the moist soil, and he pulled them out white. "Now I'll have to get a shoe shine at The Hotel Utah. Like I used to do. No wonder those people had problems. Then somewhere around here, they race cars because it's so hard."

"I read that this part is silt," I said, "and it used to be the bottom of a huge lake that once was here. That explains why it is so soft."

We stood for a few minutes staring out at the lake. In my mind, I could hear Edith Piaf, her voice ranging over the glittering salt flats...*when you kiss me heaven sighs, and though I close my eyes I see...La Vie En Rose...*

Closer to Salt Lake, we passed a sign indicating Lagoon, an amusement park that was entered from another highway. Summers we used to swim in its large, tiled swimming pool, sit on the side of the pool dangling our feet. It was from where I once watched, dazzled, as Miss Utah swam back and forth doing the breast stroke, her long blond hair drifting behind her in golden strands. Approaching the city, we went by the glittering Salt Palace, a new enormous construction used for concerts and sports. White and sparkling in the sun, it seemed to have been lifted right out of the Salt Flats.

Salt Lake was an easy city to understand. Find your way in. You had North and South Temple: South headed toward the mountains; North to the Great

Salt Lake. Intersecting was Main Street. That and State were the main streets of town We approached Main Street. There was a fancy French restaurant on a corner on the ground of what used to be—

"What was there, Lloyd, before the restaurant?"

"Well, I'll be damned. It was the Florsheim shoe store. Where I bought all my shoes. Can you beat that?"

Across from the French restaurant, on the other side of Main, was still ZCMI, the important department store owned by the Mormons.

"Something's changed about it," he said, peering across me as I drove slowly.

"I know what they did," I said, getting a better look, "they washed the front of it."

"By golly you're right. Say, you oughta go in and see if they've changed the men's department."

The men's department was where I worked at Christmas. I sold handkerchiefs, ties, and men's shirts. Pajamas was another item. I learned how to twist the ties on the front of a shirt packaged in cellophane, so it would look just like that on the husband of the wife who was thinking of buying it. For dinner, when I worked until nine, I would go downstairs to the snack shop and order a banana nut bread sandwich with cream cheese inside. Accompanying that was a nice, thick milkshake.

We continued our steady drive down Main Street. Weinstock's department store was still there, but I didn't see the Studio movie theater. There was a large sports store, so maybe it had taken over the theater. The Studio specialized in foreign films. I saw *Bitter Rice*, the first foreign movie (Italian) I had ever seen. A sign of classy progress was the new Nordstrom department store, and I wondered if that worried ZCMI.

"Look, that's where The Rainbow Rendezvous used to be." Lloyd pointed to a large movie theater on the right.

"The Rainbow Rendezvous?" In my time, it was a popular dance hall, a place I would not have recognized in daylight, even if still there. Contact lenses were not known then and myopic as I was glasses stayed in the purse on dates. I'd use them only when I combed my hair in the restroom. Vain people pay dues, and I could have been taken to a racetrack and it would have been the same for me. It had a barn-like dance hall, which was excellent for jitterbugging, and a good jitter-bugger was an important talent at The Rainbow Rendezvous that attracted a lot of the good dance bands. Dues paid by me when Nat King Cole played and sang at the piano and glasses stayed in my purse.

"Your mother and I went there once. Before you and Nina and those college dances."

"I didn't know that."

"A lot of things you didn't know. We went to hear Les Brown. Gosh, I loved to dance. I danced her all over the whole damn floor. Did I ever tell you the story of Irene Castle?"

"No. That's one I haven't heard."

"I was young, living in Chicago, out at a hotel one night with a couple of friends. In walks Irene Castle with friends—she and her husband, or brother, I don't remember, were famous ballroom dancers in my time. After they got settled at their table, I went over and asked her to dance. You know what she said?"

"What?"

"*Why, I'd be glad to.*"

I did a few turns with her on the floor, then walked her back to her table. She thanked me and told me I kept good time—and say, maybe you don't know, but your mother was a good dancer. Darn good. That night at the Rainbow Rendezvous, we danced practically the whole evening. The only time we sat down was when they played some songs from *Porgy and Bess*. They had a vocalist…what was her name…Well, I don't remember."

He began to hum, then sing some of the words to *Summertime*, a shaky, eighty-three-year-old voice, but the tune was on target. I imagined our mother dancing, floating, in Lloyd's arms around the ballroom floor. I had a flash-back of a Coke mixed with bourbon, that made me sick in The Rainbow Rendezvous restroom—myself not the only one—someone in the room recounting how she trimmed her ankles by twisting them in circles during class lectures. I remembered, too, that Lloyd had polio when a child—another story. He recovered with a small limp and yet it had never affected his dancing ability. Now here we were, in a car on streets of memories, changes in the place of old haunts. On the agenda, the cemetery.

We had not returned to the cemetery after our mother died, after we had buried her there. Distance, for the three of us, and at the same time, complicated. As a consequence, Nina, Lloyd and I had let the years pass. Closure had taken place during her burial. Memories never leaving our hearts. Now I was glad for this trip, to be able to place some flowers next to her tombstone and our father's. Somewhere along our trip, I had also convinced Lloyd, adamant he had been on not going.

We made a U-turn and went back toward the hotel. Lloyd said, "Are you going to call your friend—what's her name—who still lives in Salt Lake?"

"Jinxi? Jinxi Ralston? I don't know. I'd thought about it. Maybe I will after we get settled in the hotel."

Jinxi was my only good friend who had stayed in Salt Lake. We kept in touch. She came to Mother's funeral and had been especially kind to Lloyd that day. Ever since he had periodically asked me about her, even if he could not remember her name. Before leaving on our trip, I had considered calling her, though didn't act upon it, now I wasn't so sure. I was not in the mood for seeing anyone, while at the same time it would be good for me, the companionship of a woman friend during the bit of time we had here. These days, for that, I missed Nina.

We passed Walgreen's Drugstore, that hadn't changed, and where they sold candied pink popcorn for the movies and continued on to the hotel.

The Hotel Utah welcomed us with a deep red-wall-to-wall carpet. It spread through the vast main room—a backdrop for the modern chairs and couches in pale leather, glass coffee tables, all settled in intimate groupings to encourage conversation. Reigning were the enormous chandeliers that reflected and shimmered in crystal and brass, the lighting kept at a decent low-level. The reception desk was streamlined, and long-gone was the heavy one in what Lloyd remembered as being oak, and long-gone the welcome behind it to those who lived there while handing out the room key without asking the number. The key now a card that one slipped into a slot to open the door. Though as I reminded Lloyd, he was the one who had ended those memories having left to marry our mother. Gone was the wood and brass elevator that would fit a maximum of only five people—including the operator who in those days ran it and wore a band-box uniform. Now there were four large ones with mirrors that filled the back walls, elevators so quiet, the only way arrival was announced was upon seeing it, the door so noiseless, one didn't hear it open. No elevator operator anymore in his snappy band-box uniform.

Few changes had been made to the rooms however. His was announced by the heavy, round brass doorknob that Lloyd remembered, and had turned to open—he now estimated at least a thousand times. The key—now a card—he slipped into the slot under the doorknob.

"Ah," he exclaimed, going to the middle of the room, standing there and looking around, the first smile on his face since we had entered the hotel. "Nothing's changed. Just like my room."

I had no comment on that one because it looked as I vaguely remembered, having gone once to his room to view a parade. But hotel rooms then were not very exciting. Clean and colorless. The room we were in an example with its floral-patterned rug, two gold upholstered chairs of a matching color to the rug, a chenille bedspread in a cream color. Venetian blinds hugged the two windows. A modern addition was the new television set with remote control and a list of cable movies, a small fridge in a corner that contained beverages. Behind the bed was a large framed photograph of Salt Lake City, well done, and one could study it and come away with a good knowledge of where we were. The bathroom had smartened up. Though the tiles were still the small black and white ones that Lloyd recognized, and the toilet flushed by the old-way-steel foot- piece but stainless-steel, there was now a built-in wash-basin framed by a slick, black vinyl counter, space that held bottles of lotion and shampoo. A shower stall, elegant, framed in smoked glass was big enough for two people, which I thought modern. On a wall looking like the old-time wall telephones, but wasn't, hung an electric hair dryer.

We settled in our rooms, mine almost a carbon-copy of Lloyd's. I decided before meeting Lloyd for dinner I would call Jinxi.

Jinxi was my friend from the University of Utah. Our major was the same, therefore we had spent a great deal of time together, suffering through math classes, sharing notes in others, as well as our highly critical opinions of our professors. She was a rebel type, as rebel as one could be in the fifties. Her family was Mormon—her father held a high position in the church, her brother a missionary, and her mother a volunteer guide in the temple museum downtown. Jinxi never went to church; she smoked, drank beer, both against church rules, and her one personal vow was she would never date a missionary. Ever. She was an attractive, sultry type with a biting sense of humor, and we had shared many laughs together. Her goal was to get out of Salt Lake, travel, and later marry—maybe a foreigner. Certainly not a Mormon.

I don't know what made the turnabout in her life, only that it was after I married Dev and we had moved elsewhere. A few years later, we received an invitation to her wedding—bridegroom a missionary, and of course, they were married in the temple. They then set up their home in Salt Lake. I sent her a gift, and we continued to correspond, although she never mentioned how it came to pass she had gone against her vows. She came to Washington once for a teachers' convention and had dinner with us, but it was not the appropriate time to ask her why she had betrayed herself. I could not deny that it was also this that stimulated my interest in contacting her now: the unsolved mystery. Perhaps it was simply that she had fallen in love.

I looked her number up in the phonebook to see if it corresponded with the one I had some years ago. The name was there, but the number different. The address indicated she lived in town—a change from the Foothills, the modern suburb of Salt Lake where they lived before. As I dialed her number, it came to mind that I should have written her earlier or called from Santa Cruz instead of presenting myself without warning.

Jinxi's display of pleasure in hearing from me brought on a sense of guilt over my indecision in calling her. And it was good to hear a friend's familiar voice. We made plans to meet the next day for lunch at Trolley Square. After that I joined Lloyd downstairs in the restaurant for dinner.

"Hell, they must have gutted this whole place," he said under his breath after the waiter took our order, after placing two huge glasses of ice water on the table, that then took up a great deal of space; after he shook out the artistically folded napkins in the air with a flourish and placed them in our lap.

"For one thing," he continued, "the tables used to be bigger. Now look what they've done: made them smaller to have space for more people."

"I guess thy needed the money to cover their expenses of modernization."

"They don't need that!" His dismay about the changes turning to anger, "The church can afford it."

"I don't know, Lloyd." A mood of gloom seemed to be descending on me also. But not for the same reason. "I think I'll have a hot turkey sandwich in honor of Nina. She always ordered it here. But most of all, I'd love a glass of wine. How about you?"

"Well, that's not going to happen."

"Why not?"

"Because the restaurant is also part of the hotel, and that means part of the church, and now I'll tell you a bedtime story: no liquor is served on church property. Anybody who wants to drink has to bring their own bottle, keep it under the table."

"Oh, Lord, I forgot about that." I felt wounded, as someone who lost. I needed that drink. I craved its smoothness, the velvety texture of red wine, the cool dryness of white, the glow it gave me and after a few more sips would ease the ache that would not go away over Mike and had seemed to settle in my heart permanently, floating like a buoy.

Lloyd said, "Do you want me to go buy a bottle of wine?"

"Oh, no," the words came out in a sigh, "don't bother yourself, Lloyd."

"It's no bother. There's a liquor store right next door and not a coincidence. What do you want? Red or white?"

"Red then," recognizing my lack of any remnants of willpower.

I watched Lloyd pass among the small tables, closed in by modern chrome chairs, to go out and buy the wine. He looked mismatched in this restaurant whose décor was purple and white with stately purple and white tulips massed in vases decorating the room—Lloyd in his red and green plaid pants, a bright red handkerchief in his dark green sports jacket pocket. At one time here, he fit in. Now this was for a slick modern crowd, those who went to the theater, not the movies, who shopped at Nordstrom and did not dance anymore at the Rainbow Rendezvous because they went to the glassed Salt Palace. Someone had begun playing the piano in a corner of the room softly. I felt on the verge of weeping. I wouldn't cry. People do not cry inside serious colors of purple and white. Besides Lloyd would be back with the bottle of wine.

12.

LATE THE NEXT MORNING, I WENT OFF TO TROLLEY SQUARE TO meet Jinxi, leaving Lloyd perfectly happy to sit in the lobby of the hotel to fulfill his long-time desire of repeating the Old Days. He even thought he might take a bus to go to Ogden, a place not on the agenda but held memories for him. It was a dream, he knew he didn't mean it, he assured me after noticing alarm on my face.

Before going downstairs that morning, we called Dorrie. We had put it off until Salt Lake, feeling she might have needed time to herself to deal with what had happened. We talked about what we would say: the comforting words to find not for a death but over a dastardly crime committed by a husband. Even for Lloyd and myself, we still had not come to terms with it. We had discussed Marshall over and over in the car, and as he said earlier, even he, from his long life including Chicago memories and the gangster twenties, could not match the story. The only way was to pick up Agatha Christie, who was never choosy in where she placed the blame for a crime.

Dorrie broke down when she heard Lloyd's voice, though all he had done was greet her. But his was a fatherly figure, the consort of the motherly one, our mother, and how well I recognized the pull of maternal ties. At a loss for words, he handed me the phone. I waited for her tears to subside while mine rolled down my cheeks. Marshall, she said, having collected herself, had abused her. It had begun two years ago. She could have left him anytime, she realized this, but she loved him (not disputable when one saw them together). Much of the abuse was verbal, but there were times…She had hopes it would pass, each outburst would be the last because in *normal* periods, they had been good together. *Hope*, that's what she lived on and understands now, that only through something terrible like this would she have been able to let go. He was being brought to Santa Cruz in a couple of days…she intended to visit him…it would be hard…he has no one but her…

I could hear *vulnerability* in Dorrie's voice, words for even she knew not what, the implication that she would never learn, and even with Marshall in jail, she would pine for him. The very worst, never be able to choose a dissimilar person. She was locked in a path, *hope* ever present, false front never down. I thought of those in life capable of fooling others: Dorrie, friendly and joking in Lloyd's home—abused, welcoming me on the telephone when I arrived in Santa Cruz—abused, generously cooking all that bread for Lloyd—abused, wearing saucy earrings—abused. Going for her was her resilience, if unfortunately it seemed to be always focused in the wrong direction. Briefly and sadly, Laura's mother came to mind. Laura's own *hope* that she held in her heart.

Lloyd and I descended to the lobby of the hotel with heavy hearts.

13.

TROLLEY SQUARE WAS A BUSY MALL THAT WAS ONCE A STORAGE BARN
for trolley cars. The mall had been around for some years, and I strolled
through it to become acquainted with its new self. Abundant were restaurants
and cafes, clothing shops, also an enormous bookstore holding very informed
clerks. Colors of the mall were bright and jazzy, and it could not help but leave
most people in a good, swinging mood.

I arrived at the café before Jinxi and found a table not too far from the
entrance, so we could easily spot each other. Outside was a patio, and
people were lunching there in the warm spring sun, potted plants filled it,
and there was no music—always a gift to me when eating out, music inter-
fering with conversation. Or, when alone, with thoughts. Since the last
time I saw Jinxi was at our mother's funeral, I cannot imagine three years
would have made a difference in physical changes. After the funeral, she
had dropped us off at the motel where we were staying—myself, Nina, and
Lloyd. Jinxi, a formidable fast driver, swerved into the parking space in
front of it and fearlessly pulled to a stop. Lloyd, hand on the door handle,
couldn't wait to get out.

"Jesus Christ," he said after Jinxi drove away. Another of Jinxi's ways was
wearing ballet shoes in mid-winter. She also drank beer—equal to smoking

and forbidden by her church. I now smiled at the thought of it. Her defiance of conventions.

It was not long before I saw her in the doorway. She caught my eye, and I watched her stride toward my table, confident, thinner than before, but it looked good, hair very long, pulled back into a braid. She wore a bulky sweater over a multi-colored longish skirt.

We hugged each other.

"Margo! You look wonderful. Younger! Life obviously agrees with you." I exchanged the compliment, done honestly, for she did have the same sultry looks as before but now never looked happier.

We sat down, and for a while, even forgot to order. I don't know whose revelations were more stunning to the other: mine and my divorce with Dev, without mentioning my reason, and of course, the crime in Santa Cruz, or Jinxi's disclosure she was gay—lesbian. And as it was proper for her to overtly display shock over mine, I felt I should be more reserved—show sophistication and worldliness toward her and what these days to be gay only a revelation.

"I'm surprised you don't look more surprised," Jinxi said.

"Thank you. Your comment shows I've been successful in hiding it. I was trying to act a bit jaded."

"That's usually the reaction of most people, whereas deep down they're curious over a glass of wine: when did I know? Yes, questions like that, as if I woke up one morning...So shoot—you must have questions."

"My gosh," I said, "you've taken me off guard with your being so frank. Okay. I can finally ask the question that I have wanted to all these years: why did you go against your vows? Why did you marry a Mormon and all that went with it? You were so adamantly against anything that had to do with the church years ago."

At that moment, the waitress came, and we had to discuss the menu. I was afraid Jinxi would change the subject afterwards, not wanting to answer. I would forever not know.

After we decided on lunch, she said, "I really meant that vow at the time. It meant so much that I decided to punish myself and marry a Mormon." She smiled, "A shrink helped me find that out. You'll be surprised to know," she went on, "that I had an affair with a woman—while you and I were still in college. That was the beginning. She wasn't a student, she was a hairdresser downtown. We used to ride the bus together sometimes. She lived in our neighborhood but not close enough where others could know about us. She was older. I hated myself for it. After a while, we went our separate ways, but I was left in a kind of no-man's land. If you knew how I envied your being so normal."

"Jinxi, if someone knocked me over the head with it, then I would not have believed it. There was nothing about you that seemed gay."

Jinxi gave me a look. "Don't believe in clichés, Margo, otherwise you will not sound jaded. Anyway I finally reached a point of having to face my real feelings." She stopped a moment, then said quietly, "Or not. So I went one better by taking the straight path and marrying Graham, a Mormon—as you said, subscribed to what went with it. Somehow in my mind, I thought by doing that, joining the fold, becoming conservative, my other feelings would all go away. A cleansing. My shrink had other ideas. I was punishing myself, he said, and what a better way than self-betrayal."

"During these past days, I've come to believe nothing is reasonable anymore," I said. "What happened to Graham?"

"For Graham the whole thing had been pretty awful. You can imagine" She played with her knife and fork, set them together in various designs. "For us both. I was not happy in the marriage, and after some time, I had another affair. It doesn't even matter who she was because it didn't last long, but it pushed me to the other side. One important thing was The Womens Movement and being true to ourselves, face up to who we are. Only Graham would have stuck it out—his parents, my own, because none of them knew I was gay at the time. Just unhappy." She stopped, waiting for the waitress to finish arranging our lunch in front of us.

"It used to be," she continued, "I was concerned about making others happy. Everybody happy. Then I said to myself, hey, I'm no saint, what do I get out of this? So we split. Margo," her eyes filled with sorrow, "if you only knew what I would have given for a good marriage. But Graham and Dev have come out well. Dev married, as you said, and Graham also. Once Graham had set his mind on the failure of our marriage, it didn't take him long to find someone else. At least the wake we left was filled in. My own family now supports me. My mother," she laughed, "head guide in the Mormon church, even attends meetings with me—lesbian groups. I have a lover now, going on three years. I believe it will last. Our interests are very much the same. I'm happy as I'll ever be, and how many can say that? I don't expect more. She teaches school, like you, I work in a local library, we ski, go camping…Important we're not burdened with kids." Her voice saddened, "How is Lloyd? Your mom's passing must have been hard on him."

"Lloyd is doing well. He's fallen back into those years of being a bachelor. You might say it was good training. Makes me think I have to re-group ideas—Nina and I have been wanting to convince him to move by one of us. He's eighty-three. He's not ready to talk about it. I had hoped this trip to Salt Lake would find the moment, but we were side-tracked." I laughed, "I think during these past days, he's even enjoyed the excitement. At the same time, he's shown a lot of courage."

"My God, you've had a lot condensed in such a short amount of time."

"Do you think it was delayed punishment for allowing my marriage to fall apart?" I was joking and not joking. I had not told Jinxi about Mike. It was too painful, a wound I did not want to even think about, let alone discuss.

"You're asking the wrong person, remember? I'm the one who was into self-punishment. You left because you could not stay. That must have been very difficult." She reached over and squeezed my arm, "You'll find someone just like Dev and Graham did. As I have. So you, too, will be fine." Her grip was warm and firm.

We finished our lunch, lingered over coffee, and covered other territory: school days, people we knew, what had happened to them, some divorced, others with kids and still married, a few who we had lost track of, someone else who'd turned to booze. Life was good, and life was not always so. We summed it up that way. Obvious: always true. We promised to keep in touch, and I knew both of us would hold to that promise.

Jinxi left me in the mall because there was a store I wanted to go to. It was called *The Sound Store*, huge and well-organized. If I didn't find it there, I wouldn't find it anywhere. And I did. I even had the choice of English or French. As I waited in line to pay, I looked around remembering what it was like when I was a teenager and bought music. Then we were able to sit in a booth and test the records. If we liked one ,we bought it; if we didn't, we gave it back—never mind how scratched we might have made it—and if we only wanted to listen to music, we would pretend we wanted to buy it, go to the booth, listen for an hour or so, then return it. After that—guiltless—we'd go to Walgreen's and get a milkshake. I wondered if the cassette was in good condition. If it wasn't, it probably served me right for the Frankie Laine or Peggy Lee records we listened to and never purchased

I slipped Edith Piaf, English version, into my purse. This time after buying it. I knew I would make myself miserable, but I felt it was equal to the memory those three minutes provided for me.

The sun and warm spring air was our friend and companion the following last day. The gentle air was not for malls but as the rightful accompaniment to our "Going Back."

Lloyd found the old MGM office building still standing, now with beaded curtains in the windows, having been turned into a Turkish restaurant. Sometimes he would take us to the small theater inside, used for a screening, and where I viewed the first three-dimensional film before it was released. The special cardboard glasses gave depth to the scenes, giving the sensation of being able to touch the actors—a fad that passed quickly, the whole business uncomfortable and awkward along with the effect of making the audience very curious-looking. It was there I saw Lawrence Olivier in Hamlet.

From town a long avenue passed straight up to the mouth of a canyon— *Emigration Canyon.* I thought of it now in a new way after Mike described the whole tragedy as we sat in the car. One can imagine, or cannot, how it must have been for both parties when they emerged and viewed the valley of Salt Lake, the sweeping view below them of what was then desert. For the Donner Party, it was only time-out before continuing on; for the Mormons, it was home. What did it look like then, I wondered: flat desert-like-land, empty, with the irony of it surrounded almost completely by mountains. Mountains they probably hoped to have seen the last of after their arrival. How the women did it, I questioned, their dresses long, hampering their movements. The Mormons built a monument on the site where they emerged to commemorate their arrival. It is Brigham Young standing tall and pointing down at what must have been certainly welcoming as far as space went, who was to have stated, *This Is The Place.* Hence *This Is The Place* monument. Unfortunately for Brigham Young and his party, it became, in my time, also another *The Place*—lengthened-dates in cars, in lieu of not going right home. But I suspect Brigham Young would not have been insulted, he with more than one wife at the same time. Now there was also a small museum, a gift shop, and an information center and employees dressed as pioneers to answer questions. We stopped for a moment to admire the view of the city that spread out below.

"Margo," Lloyd said, "when I leave this world, I want to be cremated. I want my ashes scattered from here."

"Okay, Lloyd."

There was nothing else to say. Nina and I would do that.

Our house was on a side-street close by. The same yellow brick, the pine tree in front, taller, pink and red tulips were in full bloom in the flower beds and the driveway, to the garage, re-surfaced an even shiny black. It had *earned* a new face. Many times—before Lloyd—the three of us had shoveled the snow from it to release our car.

When Lloyd entered our family, he acquired also the title of gardener, a role as foreign to him as it would have been for our mother to pass her days going back and forth through the lobby of the Hotel Utah. I suspect he liked it more than not, proof being he spent a lot of time doing it.

"Do you remember the walking sprinkler we had, Lloyd?"

"Sure I remember. The damn thing used to walk along the hose while it watered and every once in a while get stuck and gouge out the lawn. Other than that, it was a good invention for those who didn't have a sprinkling system like us. Your mother loved flowers," he said. As we sat in the car staring at the house, "But those damn roses I planted in the backyard. They were the bane of my existence. Always full of disease or bugs, always had to spray them."

"You did that for her," I said, then eyed him cautiously, my outburst of sentiment maybe causing him discomfort.

He didn't seem to notice for he was caught up with his own thoughts, not able to tear his eyes from the house. I, too, had mine, pictures, scenes: pigeons, beautiful white pouter pigeons—an idea of our grandfather's who had constructed an elaborate cage for them; our mother humming while she cooked— in high-heeled shoes. Nina and I dressing up for Easter, gardenia corsages waiting in the icebox; the ice rink next door our neighbor made in his backyard by filling up the homemade badminton court; the icy wind that blew down from the canyon behind us in winter time and whistled around the sides of the house; the hateful walks back home in the snow from school; Lloyd and our mother dressed up to go out, she in a long, sky-blue dress that matched the color of her eyes.

I looked over at Lloyd. He was still staring at the house. "Lloyd," I said, gently. "Lloyd...I think we better go. People in the house might wonder why we're stopped here so long in front of it."

For a moment, he looked startled, puzzled as to where he was. He bowed his head and stared at his hands gripping the base of the steering wheel. And in the quiet, I waited. Then he reached up and turned the key to start the car.

On the way to town, Lloyd said, "This is where Mrs. Ogden used to live. On one of those streets. For years, when I lived in the hotel, she washed and ironed my shirts. Every Saturday I would drop them off and pick them up the next Saturday. They were ten very nice shirts. And if a button was loose, she would fix it. After I married your mother, Mrs. Ogden still did my shirts. Every Saturday. She lived in a small house. A very kind lady. Gone now she was older than I was. I would see her at the door and give them to her and see her at the door when I picked them up. I paid her once a month. She seemed the same age during all those years. Never knew her husband. Never saw the inside of her house. Your mother never met her. She was just Mrs. Ogden, who always washed and ironed my shirts."

I said, "The name existed among the four of us: Mrs. Ogden. A Saturday name. One who belonged to Saturdays. Sometimes you would say you were leaving now for Mrs. Ogden's. My picture of her always the same as her weekly Saturdays—grey hair, a small person with talented hands that perfectly ironed your shirts."

He laughed, "You missed that one because she was tall. "

I left Lloyd in the lobby of the hotel to watch people and went up to Alta, the ski area forty minutes from town. There was still snow, people were spring skiing, lines waiting to get on the chair lift. I walked around the bottom of the main ski lift in my new Truckee boots, stood and watched the skiers come down. Now I was a stranger here, a tourist, and it felt odd. I had buddies then that I skied with—or didn't because, if one thinks of it, the act of skiing is a lone sport. Buddies. Dispersed all of them, like myself, where in the town I live the mountains not as close. The Sierra. I thought of *her*, readying to take on spring; how pleased *she* must be to show *her* colors. I thought of the mountains, the living creations they are. They holding abuse, deep scars, litter, from us skiers and those who climb, we who had used them for entertainment. I thought of avalanches, their defense. I thought of our trip soon to end, my life as a teacher I would return to. A good feeling but not for the same person. But one with a new hair style—and I smiled at that, it's metaphor for change. I thought of Salt Lake. It had given us four a happy life in that yellow brick house, and it had left its light in me and now, at this moment, while looking up at *my* mountain, there were the joys it allowed, as Mike's gave him. Yes, life is full, it has a light to follow it. For me it took our trip to know this.

I went into the lodge and bought a beer. The air was steamy and warm and reminded me of Bud's, the diner where Mike and I had lunch. The air held also the aroma of onions and hamburgers—a fit combination as another reminder. The beer was good, icy cold. I took it outside, found a place to sit in the sun, and nursed it.

We had planned to go to the cemetery, and I picked Lloyd up on my way back from Alta. First we stopped at the florist and bought a large bouquet of daisies. He wasn't keen on the choice, but I told him they'd outlast roses.

"We won't be back for a while, remember that." This statement quieted him. They would do. We could imagine daisies sitting in their vase, still pert long after we left. This was their reputation, I assured him. They will last.

It took some time to find the gravesite, but it wasn't unpleasant following the tree-lined windy roads that led through the simple, well-kept cemetery; the last afternoon air was cooling, the sun a deeper yellow.

"I think it's under the group of trees over there," Lloyd called back, for I was lagging due to my ski boots that I should have changed. We had parked the car and were finding our way by foot.

I picked up my steps, and we headed in that direction. The day of the funeral, we got lost—as now—Nina, Lloyd and I. Nina was driving our rented car: backing up, going forward again, taking uncertain side roads. It all seemed impossible at the time, that we, lost creatures, had the goal of our mother's, wife's burial.

"There it is, Lloyd, near the corner, under the tree." I purposefully left out *they* because next to her was our father's tombstone, and I had uncertain feelings about facing the two of them with Lloyd. I had never mentioned our father in Lloyd's presence, and now it seemed the four of us, two in death, were the only ones in the world. I quickly took the daisies from their wrapping, and we knelt down and arranged them in the vase that was set in front of our mother's gravestone. Lloyd fetched water from a near-by faucet, a bucket there to carry it in. While he was gone, I carefully arranged some of the daisies in the vase in front of the tombstone of my father. When Lloyd came back with the water, he poured it in both of the vases. Done, we stood back and admired our work in silence. The flowers looked bright and cheerful. I watched them nod, swing their heads in the light breeze, they the appointed long-lasting caretakers. I thought of Lloyd's choice, of his remains in flight across the desert of Salt Lake…

"You know what I think?" I said, driving back to the hotel.

"I can't imagine."

"I think you should marry Junie."

He glanced over at me, and I could almost feel the surprised expression on his face.

"Oh, I don't know," he said quietly, having collected himself. "There's you and Nina. I don't want to do anything that would…your mother…"

"I think it would be great, and I know Nina would agree. And you know something? I know Mother would agree. Junie was her good friend. You're both alone."

"You really feel that way?"

"I really do, Lloyd."

"You'd come to the wedding?"

"How can you ask that? We would bring bells, Lloyd."

"What if there was no wedding?" he said suddenly. He looked over at me slyly, a smile on his face.

"So you meant it when you asked my opinion about Junie moving in with you? You didn't mean marriage? What are you, becoming modern or something?"

"Could be," he said, "could be."

"What would they say, all you neighbors?" I said half joking.

"Oh, dammit, let them talk."

"Do you really mean it?"

"Sure I do. We're adult people."

I looked over at him and laughed. He laughed, too.

We passed through the suburbs, then along The Avenues, the area of old, elegant homes. The cottonwoods were in bloom, and the breeze carried their fragile, white petals through the air, against the windshield of the car and into patterns on the sidewalks.

At our last meal in the dining room of The Hotel Utah, we were both ready to leave. Lloyd had not pronounced it, but we had done what we had come to do. We had taken care of memories, put them away for safekeeping, wondered at so many changes, and that was as it should be, to be expected. At the end of the meal, a waiter came to the table and politely told Lloyd there was a telephone call for him at the front desk.

"That's Nina," I said as he got up. How I missed her this trip.

We still had some wine left, and I reached under the table to bring the bottle up. I finished it, pouring it in both our glasses. Tonight the piano was playing jazz. Nice soft jazz, slow not intrusive. Listening I took slow sips of the wine. Tomorrow we would make our stopover on the outskirts of Reno, then next day to Santa Cruz. I wondered what it would be like in the compound after Marshall. Stories we would probably hear over and over again. I thought, poor Lloyd, but on the other hand, a good story for his repertoire. I would leave some days later, my vacation ended.

I looked up and saw Lloyd returning. He had a light spring to his step that always foretold of something good. He sat down. He reached into his jacket pocket for a cigar, kept for after-dinner-occasions. Prepared it for a light. Lit it. Drew on it and blew the smoke out. I always liked the slight pungent smell of his cigar, and smoking was not forbidden in the dining room.

"That was Mike on the phone. He's fine. He was released from the hospital yesterday. He's at the hotel for a couple of nights, in a room Hank and Sally gave him. He asked us if we could stop there on our way back instead of Reno." He drew again on his cigar, it brightened, then softened. I waited because it seemed he had something else to say.

"He asked me what I thought of his coming to visit you in Washington. Testing the water with *me*, you might say. Do you want to know what I told him?"

"Yes," I said softly.

"I said, Mike, if you have made good decisions in your life, then going to Washington would be the best one. I told him that we'd see him, tomorrow, in Truckee. I hope you don't mind my answering for you."

He reached over and pat my hand, then drew seriously on the cigar, and the smoke drifted in front of us, the cigar sending out more of its subtle aroma.

I watched the smoke, it curled and drifted through the golds and purples in the room while the jazz played quietly from a corner…

"Okay, Toots, to another show on the road." He raised his glass of red wine.

A name for Nina and myself and special occasions.

THE END